Lady, lady, I did it!

Ed McBain was born in Manhattan, but fled to the Bronx at the age of twelve. He went through elementary and high school in the New York school system, and the Navy claimed him in 1944. When he returned two years later, he attended Hunter College. After a variety of jobs, he worked for a literary agent, where he learnt about plotting stories. When his agent-boss started selling them regularly to magazines, and sold a mystery novel and a juvenile science-fiction title as well, they both decided that it would be more profitable for him to stay at home and write full time.

Under his own name, Evan Hunter, he is the author of a number of novels, including *The Blackboard Jungle*, *Come Winter* and *Every Little Crook and Nanny*. As Ed McBain he has written the highly popular '87th Precinct' series of crime novels, including *Shotgun*, *Jigsaw*, *Fuzz*, *Hail, Hail, the Gang's All Here!* and *Sadie When She Died*, all of which are available in Pan.

Ed McBain

Lady, lady, I did it!

An 87th Precinct Mystery

Pan Books London and Sydney

First published in Great Britain 1980 by Pan Books Ltd,
Cavaye Place, London SW10 9PG
© Ed McBain 1961
ISBN 0 330 26095 2
Set, printed and bound in Great Britain by
Cox & Wyman Ltd, Reading

This is for Henry Morrison

1

Patterns

The pattern of October sunlight filtering past barred and grilled windows to settle in an amber splash on a scarred wooden floor. Shadows merge with the sun splash – the shadows of tall men in shirt sleeves; this is October, but the squad room is hot and Indian summer is dying slowly.

A telephone rings.

There is the sound of a city beyond those windows. The sudden shriek in unison of children let out from school, the pedlar behind his cart – 'Hot dogs, orange drink' – the sonorous rumble of buses and automobiles, the staccato click of high-heeled pumps, the empty rattle of worn roller skates on chalked sidewalks. Sometimes the city goes suddenly still. You can almost hear a heartbeat. But this silence is a part of the city noise, a part of the pattern. In the stillness, sometimes a pair of lovers will walk beneath the windows of the squad room, and their words will drift upward in a whispered fade. A cop will look up from his typewriter. A city is going by outside.

Patterns.

A detective is standing at the water cooler. He holds the cone-shaped paper cup in his hand, waits until it is filled, and then tilts his head back to drink. A .38 Police Special is resting in a holster which is clipped to the lefthand side of his belt. A typewriter is going across the room, hesitantly, fumblingly, but reports must be typed, and in triplicate; cops do not have private secretaries.

Another phone rings.

'87th Squad, Carella.'

There is a timelessness to this room. There are patterns overlapping patterns, and they combine to form the classic design that is police work. The design varies slightly from day to day. There is an office routine, and an investigatory routine, and very rarely does a case come along which breaks the classic pattern. Police work is like a bullfight. There is always a ring, and always a bull, and always a matador and picadors and chulos, and always, too, the classic music of the arena, the opening trumpet playing *La Virgen de la Macarena*, the ritual music throughout, announcing the various stages of a contest which is not a contest at all. Usually the bull dies. Sometimes, but only when he is an exceptionally brave bull, he is spared. But for the most part he dies. There is no real sport involved here because the outcome is assured before the mock combat begins. The bull will die. There are, to be sure, some surprises within the framework of the sacrificial ceremony – a matador will be gored, a bull will leap the *barrera* – but the pattern remains set and unvaried, the classic ritual of blood.

It is the same with police work.

There are patterns to this room. There is a timelessness to these men in this place doing the work they are doing.

They are all deeply involved in the classic ritual of blood.

'87th Squad, Detective Kling.'

Bert Kling, youngest man on the squad, cradled the telephone receiver between his shoulder and his ear, leaned over the typewriter, and began erasing a mistake. He had misspelled 'apprehended'.

'Who?' he said into the phone. 'Oh, sure, Dave, put her on.' He waited while Dave Murchison, manning the switchboard in the muster room downstairs, put the call through.

From the water cooler, Meyer Meyer filled another paper cup and said, 'He's always got a girl on the phone. The girls in this city, they got nothing else to do, they call Detective Kling and ask him how the crime is going today.' He shook his head.

Kling shushed him with an outstretched palm. 'Hello, honey,' he said into the phone.

'Oh, it's *her*,' Meyer said knowingly.

Steve Carella, completing a call at his own desk, hung up and said, 'It's who?'

'Who do you think? Kim Novak, that's who. She calls here every day. She wants to know should she buy some stock in Columbia Pictures.'

'Will you guys please shut up?' Kling said. Into the phone, he said, 'Oh, the usual. The clowns are at it again.'

Claire Townsend, on the other end of the line, said, 'Tell them to stop kibitzing. Tell them we're in love.'

'They already know that,' Kling said. 'Listen, are we all set for tonight?'

'Yes, but I'll be a little late.'

'Why?'

'I've got a stop to make after school.'

'What kind of a stop?' Kling asked.

'I have to pick up some texts. Stop being suspicious.'

'Why don't you stop being a schoolgirl?' Kling asked. 'Why don't you marry me?'

'When?'

'Tomorrow.'

'I can't tomorrow. I'll be very busy tomorrow. Besides, the world needs social workers.'

'Never mind the world. *I* need a wife. I've got holes in my socks.'

'I'll darn them when I get there tonight,' Claire said.

'Well, actually,' Kling whispered, 'I had something else in mind.'

'He's whispering,' Meyer said to Carella.

'Shut up,' Kling said.

'Every time he gets to the good part, he whispers,' Meyer said, and Carella burst out laughing.

'This is getting impossible,' Kling said, sighing. 'Claire, I'll see you at six-thirty, OK?'

'Seven's more like it,' she said. 'I'm wearing a disguise, by the way. So your nosy landlady won't recognize me when she peeks into the hall.'

'What do you mean? What kind of a disguise?'

'You'll see.'

'No, come on. What are you wearing?'

'Well . . . I've got on a white blouse,' Claire said, 'open at the throat, you know, with a strand of very small pearls. And a black skirt, very tight, with a wide black belt, the one with the silver buck . . .'

As she spoke, Kling smiled unconsciously, forming a mental picture of her in the university phone booth. He knew she would be leaning over very close to the mouthpiece. She was five feet seven inches tall, and the booth would seem too small for her. Her hair, as black as sin, would be brushed back from her face, her brown eyes intensely alive as she spoke, perhaps with a faint smile on her mouth. The full white blouse would taper to a narrow waist, the black skirt hanging on wide hips, dropping in a straight line over her thighs and her long legs.

'... no stockings because the weather's so damn hot,' Claire said, 'and high-heeled black pumps, and that's it.'

'So, where's the disguise?'

'Well, I bought a new bra,' Claire whispered.

'Oh?'

'You should see what it does for me, Bert.' She paused. 'Do you love me, Bert?'

'You know I do,' he said.

'She just asked him does he love her,' Meyer said, and Kling pulled a face.

'Tell me,' Claire whispered.

'I can't right now.'

'Will you tell me later?'

'Mmmm,' Kling said, and he glanced apprehensively at Meyer.

'Wait until you see this bra,' Claire said.

'Yes, I'm looking forward to it,' Kling said, watching Meyer, phrasing his words carefully.

'You don't sound very interested,' Claire said.

'I am. It's a little difficult, that's all.'

'It's called "Abundance",' Claire said.

'What is?'

'The bra.'

'That's nice,' Kling said.

'What are they doing up there? Standing around your desk and breathing down your neck?'

'Well, not exactly, but I think I'd better say good-bye now. I'll see you at six-thirty, honey.'

'Seven,' Claire corrected.

'OK. 'Bye, doll.'

'Abundance,' she whispered, and she hung up. Kling put the receiver back into the cradle.

'OK,' he said, 'I'm going to call the telephone company and ask them to put in a phone booth.'

'You're not supposed to make private calls on the city's time,' Carella said, and he winked at Meyer.

'I didn't *make* this call. I *received* it. Also, a man is entitled to a certain amount of privacy, even if he works with a bunch of horny bastards. I don't see why I can't talk to my fiancée without—'

'He's sore,' Meyer said. 'He called her his fiancée instead of his girl. Look, talk to her. Call her back and tell her you sent all us gorillas out of the room and now you can talk to her. Go ahead.'

'Go to hell,' Kling said. Angrily, he turned back to his type-writer, forgetting that he'd been in the middle of an erasure. He began typing again and then realized he was overscoring what he'd already typed. Viciously, he ripped the almost-completed report from the machine. 'See what you made me do?' he shouted impotently. 'Now I have to start all over again!' He shook his head despairingly, took a white, a blue, and a yellow Detective Division Report from his top drawer, separated the three sheets with carbon paper, and began typing again, bang-ing the keys with a vengeance.

Steve Carella walked to the window and looked down to the street below. He was a tall man, and he stood in slender de-ceptive grace by the meshed grille, the late afternoon sunlight washing over him, his angular body giving no clue to the de-structive power in his muscular arms and chest. In profile, he looked slightly oriental, the sun limning high cheekbones and eyes that slanted curiously downward.

'This time of day,' he said, 'I feel like going to sleep.'

Meyer looked at his watch. 'That's because we'll be relieved soon,' he said.

Across the room, Kling kept battering the typewriter keys.

There were sixteen detectives, not counting Lieutenant Byrnes, attached to the 87th Squad. Of those sixteen, four were usually on special assignment somewhere or other, leaving a twelve-man squad, which was divided into four duty sections of three-man teams. Unlike patrolmen, the detectives worked out their own schedules, and the pattern, though arbitrary, was consistent. There were two shifts, the eight a.m. to six p.m. and the six p.m. to eight a.m. The graveyard shift was the longer of the two, and none of the detectives particularly enjoyed it, but they nonetheless drew it every fourth day. They were also 'off duty' every fourth day, a term which didn't mean very much since all cops are technically 'on duty' twenty-four hours a day, every day of the year. Besides, most of the detectives on the squad found that they *needed* those off-duty days to accomplish vital legwork. The schedule was a complicated thing to keep, because the special-assignment cops kept changing, and because Lineup was held every day from Monday to Thursday and the detectives were required to put in appearances there in order to acquaint themselves with the men who were committing crimes throughout the city, and because detectives had to appear in court to testify at trials, and because – the schedule was a difficult one to keep. Teams kept changing, men kept coming and going, there were often eight cops in the squad room instead of three. The schedule was posted each week, but following it was impossible.

In any case, one thing remained constant. The relieving detectives, by unwritten agreement, always arrived at the squad room fifteen minutes before the hour, a carry-over from their patrolman days. The graveyard shift, not due until six p.m., would undoubtedly straggle in any time between five-thirty and five forty-five.

It was five-fifteen p.m. when the telephone rang.

Meyer Meyer lifted the receiver and said '87th Squad, Detective Meyer.' He moved a pad into place on his desk. 'Yeah, go ahead,' he said. He began writing on the pad. 'Yep,' he said. He wrote down an address. 'Yep.' He continued writing. 'Yep, right away.' He hung up. 'Steve, Bert,' he said, 'you want to take this?'

'What is it?' Carella asked.

12

'Some nut just shot up a bookstore on Culver Avenue,' Meyer said. 'There're three people lying dead on the floor.'

The crowd had already gathered around the bookshop. A sign out front read 'GOOD BOOKS, GOOD READING'. There were two uniformed cops on the sidewalk, and a squad car was pulled up to the kerb across the street. The people pulled back instinctively when they heard the wail of the siren on the police sedan. Carella got out first, slamming the door behind him. He waited for Kling to come around the car, and then both men started for the shop. At the door, the patrolman said, 'Lot of dead people in there, sir.'

'When'd you get here?'

'Few minutes ago. We were just cruising when we took the squeal. We called back the minute we saw what it was.'

'Know how to keep a timetable?'

'Yes, sir.'

'Come along and keep it then.'

'Yes, sir.'

They started into the shop. Not three feet from the door they saw the first body. The man was partially slumped against one of the bookstalls, partially sprawled on the floor. He was wearing a blue seersucker suit, and his hand was still holding a book, and a line of blood had run down his arm, and stained his sleeve, and continued down over the hand holding the book. Kling looked at him and knew instantly that this was going to be a bad one. Just how bad, he did not yet realize.

'Here's another one,' Carella said.

The second body was some ten feet away from the first, another man coatless, his head twisted and fitting snugly into the angle formed by the bookstall and the floor. As they approached, he moved his head slightly, trying to raise it from its uncomfortable position. A new flow of blood spilled on to his shirt collar. He dropped his head again. The patrolman, his throat parched, his voice containing something like awe, said, 'He's alive.'

Carella stooped down beside the man. The man's neck had been ripped open by the force of the bullet which had struck

13

him. Carella looked at torn flesh and muscle, and for an instant he closed his eyes, the action coming as swiftly as the clicking shutter of a camera, the eyes opening again at once, a tight hard mask claiming his face.

'Did you call for a meat wagon?' he asked.

'The minute I got here,' the patrolman said.

'Good.'

'There are two others,' a voice said.

Kling turned away from the dead man in the seersucker suit. The man who'd spoken was a small, birdlike man with a bald head. He stood crouched against one of the bookstalls, his hand to his mouth. He was wearing a shabby brown sweater open over a white shirt. There was abject terror on his face and in his eyes. He was sobbing low, muted sobs which accompanied the tears that flowed from his eyes, oddly channelling themselves along either side of his nose. As Kling approached him, he thought, Two others. Meyer said there were three. But it's four.

'Are you the owner of this shop?' he asked.

'Yes,' the man said. 'Please look at the others. Back there. Is an ambulance coming? A wild man, a wild man. Look at the others, please. They may be alive. One of them is a woman. Please look at them.'

Kling nodded and walked to the back of the shop. He found the third man bent double over one of the counters, an open book beside him; he had undoubtedly been browsing when the shots were loosed. The man was dead, his mouth open, his eyes staring sightlessly. Unconsciously, Kling's hands went to the man's eyelids. Gently he closed them.

The woman lay on the floor beside him.

She was wearing a red blouse.

She had undoubtedly been carrying an armful of books when the bullets took her. She had fallen to the floor, and the books had fallen around her and upon her. One book lay just under her extended right hand. Another, open like a tent, covered her face and her black hair. A third leaned against her curving hip. The red blouse had pulled free from the woman's black skirt as she had fallen. The skirt had risen over the backs of her long legs. One leg was bent, the other rigid and straight. A black

14

high-heeled pump lay several inches away from one naked foot. The woman wore no stockings.

Kling knelt beside her. Oddly, the titles of the books registered on his mind: *Patterns of Culture* and *The Sane Society* and *Interviewing: Its Principles and Methods*. He saw suddenly that the blouse was not a red blouse at all. A corner that had pulled free from the black skirt showed white. There were two enormous holes in the girl's side, and the blood had poured steadily from those wounds, staining the white blouse a bright red. A string of tiny pearls had broken when she had fallen, and the pearls lay scattered on the floor now, tiny luminescent islands in the sticky coagulation of her blood. He felt pain looking at her. He reached for the book which had fallen open over her face. He lifted the book, and the pain suddenly became a very personal, very involved thing.

'Oh my Jesus Christ!' he said.

There was something in his voice which caused Steve Carella to run towards the back of the shop immediately. And then he heard Kling's cry, a single sharp anguished cry that pierced the dust-filled, cordite-stinking air of the shop.

'*Claire!*'

He was holding the dead girl in his arms when Carella reached him. His hands and his face were covered with Claire Townsend's blood, and he kissed her lifeless eyes and her nose and her throat, and he kept murmuring over and over again, 'Claire, Claire,' and Steve Carella would remember that name and the sound of Kling's voice as long as he lived.

2

Detective-Lieutenant Peter Byrnes was having dinner with his wife and his son when Carella called him. Harriet, who had been a policeman's wife for a long time, knew immediately that it was someone from the squad. The men of the 87th called only when the family was in the middle of dinner. No, that wasn't quite true. They sometimes called in the middle of the night, when everyone was asleep.

She said, 'I'll get it,' and she rose from the table and walked into the foyer, where the telephone rested on the hall table. When she recognized Carella's voice, she immediately smiled. She could still remember clearly a time not so long ago when Carella had been very personally involved in a situation that had threatened the entire Byrnes family. While investigating the case, Carella had been shot in Grover Park by a narcotics pedlar, and she could remember that long Christmas Eve vigil when it seemed he would die. He had lived, and now when she heard his voice she smiled immediately and unconsciously, as if constantly pleased and surprised and grateful for his presence.

'Harriet,' he said, 'may I talk to Pete, please?'

There was an undertone of urgency to his voice. She said simply, 'Of course, Steve,' and walked instantly from the phone and into the dining room. She said, 'It's Steve.'

Byrnes pushed back his chair. He was a compact man who moved economically, his movements seeming to be a direct translation of thought into energy. The chair went back, his napkin came down on to the table, he moved briskly and rapidly to the phone, picked up the receiver, spoke the instant it was close to his mouth.

'Yeah, Steve?'

'Pete, I . . . I . . .'

'What's the matter?'

'Pete . . .'

'What is it, Steve?'

There was a silence on the other end of the line. For a moment Byrnes thought Carella was . . . crying? He held the phone close to his ear, listening, waiting. A slight tic began near his left eye.

'Pete, I'm . . . I'm at a bookshop on Culver and . . . and . . .'

There was a pause. Byrnes waited. He could hear Carella asking someone where the bookshop was. He could hear a muffled voice giving Carella the information.

16

'North Forty-ninth,' Carella said into the phone. 'The name is The Brow . . . The Browser. That's the name of the shop, Pete.'

'All right, Steve,' Byrnes said. Still he waited.

'Pete, I think you better come down here.'

'All right, Steve,' Byrnes said. Still he waited.

'Pete, I . . . I can't handle this right now. Kling is . . . Pete, this is a terrible thing.'

'What happened?' Byrnes asked gently.

'Somebody came in . . . and . . . sh . . . shot up the store. Kl . . . Kl . . . Kl . . . Kl . . .'

He could not get the word out. The stammering filled the line like subdued machine-gun fire. *Click, click, click, click*, and Byrnes waited. There was silence.

In a rush, Carella said, 'Kling's girl was here. She's dead.'

Byrnes caught his breath in a quick, small rush. 'I'll be right there,' he said, and he hung up rapidly. For a moment, he felt only intense relief. He had expected worse: he had expected injury to Carella's wife or children. But the relief was short-lived because it was followed immediately by guilt. Kling's girl, he thought, and he tried to construct an image of her; but he'd never met her. And yet she seemed real to him because he had heard the squad-room jokes about Kling's romance with the young social worker, the corny goddamn squad-room jokes . . . she was dead . . . Kling . . .

There.

There was the thing. His first concern had been for Carella, because he looked upon him as the eldest son in a family business. But now he thought of Kling, young and blond and wide-eyed in a business where you could not flinch.

Byrnes did not want to think this way. I'm a cop, he told himself; I run a squad, I'm the boss, I'm the skipper, I'm the old man, they call me the old man. I can't, I can't, I *can't* get involved with the personal lives of the men on that squad, I am not their father, goddamn it!

But he strapped on his gun, and he put on his hat, and he kissed Harriet and touched his real son, Larry, on the shoulder, and there was a troubled and concerned look on his face as he went out of the house because he *was* involved with these men, had been involved with them for a long time now, and maybe this involvement did not make him a better cop, but it most certainly made him a better man.

There were six detectives from the 87th waiting outside the bookshop when Byrnes got there. Meyer Meyer had been relieved and had brought two men from the oncoming graveyard shift with him. Cotton Hawes and Andy Parker had been off duty, but the catcher on the graveyard shift had called to tell them what had happened, and they had rushed over to the bookstore. Bob O'Brien had been on special assignment in a barber's shop four blocks away when a patrolman had brought him the news. He had run all the way to the bookstore.

The men stood on the sidewalk uneasily as Byrnes got out of his car. Two of the men had every right to be there since they were technically manning the squad room. The rest were there voluntarily, and they stood in the slightly stupid posture of volunteers everywhere, not sure why they were there, waiting for someone to tell them what to do. Two Homicide cops were outside with them, smoking, chatting with the police photographer. An ambulance was at the kerb and four patrol cars blocked the street. A dozen patrolmen were on the sidewalk, trying to keep back curious onlookers. A few reporters who had been hanging out in the wire room opposite Headquarters downtown had got the flash from the dispatcher manning the police radio and had come racing uptown to see what all the shouting was about.

Meyer broke away from the knot of men the moment he saw the lieutenant. He walked to him quickly and fell into step beside him.

'Where's Steve?' Byrnes asked.

'Inside.'

'And Bert?'

'I sent him home.'

'How is he?'

'How would you be?' Meyer asked, and Byrnes nodded. 'I had to force him to leave. I sent two patrolmen with him. The girl . . . ah, Pete, this is a mess.'

They stood to one side as a pair of ambulance attendants went past with a man on a stretcher.

'That's the last one,' Meyer said. 'One of them was still alive when they got here. Don't know how long he'll be that way. The M.E. thinks his spine was shattered.'

'How many altogether?' Byrnes asked.

'Four. Three dead.'

'Was . . . was Kling's girl . . .?'

'Yeah. Dead when they got here.'

Byrnes nodded briefly. Before he went into the bookstore, he said, 'Tell O'Brien he's supposed to be in that barber's shop. Tell the others to go home; we'll call them if we need them. Whose squeal is this, Meyer?'

'It came in about a half hour before relief. You want us to stay on it?'

'Who relieved?'

'Di Maeo, Brown, and Willis.'

'Where's Di Maeo?'

'Back at the squad, catching.'

'Tell Willis and Brown to stick around. Did you have anything important for tonight?'

'No. I'd like to call Sarah, though.'

'Can you stay around for a while?'

'Sure.'

'Thanks,' Byrnes said, and he went into the shop.

The bodies were gone. Only their chalked outlines remained on the floor and on the bookstalls. Two men from the police laboratory were dusting the shop for latent prints. Byrnes looked around for Carella and then thought of something. He went quickly to the door of the shop.

'Willis!' he said.

Hal Willis moved away from the men on the sidewalk. He was a small man, barely clearing the five-foot-eight height requirement for policemen. He walked with graceful precision, a small-boned man who had devoted half his life to the study and practice of judo, a man constantly aware of weight and balance, an awareness which showed in every move he made. He came up alongside the lieutenant and said, 'Yeah, Pete?'

'I want you to get over to the hospital. Take Brown with you. See if you can get anything from that man who's still alive.'

'Right, Pete.'

'He's in a bad way,' Byrnes said. 'A dying declaration is admissible in court – remember that.'

'Yeah,' Willis said. 'Which hospital?'

'Meyer knows. Ask him.'

'Anything else?'

'Not for now. If they won't let you see him, raise a stink. Call me at the squad if you get anything. I'll be there.'

'Right.'

Byrnes went into the shop again. Steve Carella was sitting on a high stool in one corner of the shop. His hands, clasped together, were dangling between his knees. He was staring at the floor when Byrnes approached him.

'Steve?'

He nodded.

'You all right?'

He nodded again.

'Come on.'

'What?'

'Come on; snap out of it.'

Carella raised his head. His eyes were dead. He looked straight at Byrnes, and straight through him.

'This is a lousy rotten job,' he said.

'All right, it's—'

DETECTIVE DIVISION REPORT	SQUAD	PRECINCT	PRECINCT REPORT NUMBER	DETECTIVE DIVISION REPORT NUMBER
PDCN 360 REV. 25M	87	87°	32-41	D.D. 74 R-11

NAME AND ADDRESS OF PERSON REPORTING	DATE OF REPORT
Fennerman, Martin (N.M.I.)	October 13

SURNAME GIVEN NAME INITIALS	
Browser Bookshop 2680 Culver Avenue	Isola

| NUMBER STREET | CITY SECTION |

Details
Martin Fennerman is owner and operator

20

of The Browser, a bookstore located at address above. Home address 375 Harris Street in Riverhead. Fennerman is forty-seven years old, divorced; two children living with remarried wife, Olga (Mrs Ira) Trent in Bethtown. Fennerman has owned and operated bookshop at above location for twelve years. Store was held up in 1954, thief apprehended, see D.D. Report #41 F-38, sentenced Castleview, released good behaviour January, 1956, returned to home in Denver, respectably employed there.

Mr Fennerman states as follows:

The shop is open every day but Sunday. He comes to work at nine in the morning, closes at six except on Saturday when he stays open until eight p.m. Except for the holdup in 1954, he has never had any trouble at this location, even though neighbourhood is not ideal for bookshop. There were seven people in the shop this evening when the killer entered. Mr Fennerman keeps count of the people as they come in. He sits behind a high counter just inside the entrance doorway, checks out purchases as customers leave. There is a cash register on the counter, paper bags for wrapping purchases under the counter. Fennerman's system of keeping count was designed to avoid petty theft, he says. In any case, there were seven people in the store when the killer came in. Fennerman says this was at five-ten p.m. One of the stray bullets shattered clock on rear wall of shop, stopping it at five-seven p.m. According to Fennerman, the killer began shooting the moment he entered the shop, so ETA would be five-five or five-six.

The man was tall, perhaps six feet, perhaps more. He was wearing a tweed

overcoat, a grey fedora, sunglasses,
black gloves. Fennerman especially
remembers the black gloves. He thinks
the overcoat may have been blue, but he
is not certain. The killer came into the
store with his hands in his pockets,
stopped just beyond the cash register,
pulled his hands from his pockets, and
began firing. He carried two guns. He
kept shooting into the aisle of the shop
until both guns were empty, Fennerman
says, and then turned and ran out. He said
nothing to Fennerman and nothing to any
of the patrons. The four people he shot
were standing in the aisle running back
from the cash register. The other three
people in the store were in the other
aisle, to the left of the entrance.
Fennerman says none of them even knew
what was happening until it was all over.
One of the women fainted as the killer
ran out. Names and disposition of the
seven people in the store at time of
killing follow, exclusive of Fennerman.

Claire Townsend	DOA
Anthony La Scala	DOA
Herbert Land	DOA
Joseph Wechsler	Hospitalized – Neck Wound
Myra Klein	Hospitalized – Shock
Barbara Deering	Returned to residence
James Woody	Returned to residence

DATE OF THIS REPORT

October 13

RANK	SURNAME	INITIALS	SHIELD NUMBER	COMMAND
Det-Lt.	Byrnes	P. A.	681	87th Squad.

Detective - Lieutenant Peter A. B

SIGNATURE OF COMMANDING OFFICER

'I don't want it, I don't *want* it,' Carella said, his voice rising. 'I want to go home and touch my kids and not have blood on my hands.'

'All right—'

'I don't want the stink of it!' Carella shouted.

'Nobody does! Snap out of it!'

'Snap out of *what*? Of seeing that poor damn girl lying twisted and broken and bleeding on the floor? Of Bert holding her in his arms, covered with blood, and rocking her, rocking her ... Jesus *Christ*!'

'Nobody asked you to be a cop,' Byrnes said.

'You're goddamn right, nobody asked me! OK. *OK!* Nobody asked.' His eyes had filled with tears. He sat on the high stool with his hands clasped tightly together, as if he were clinging to his sanity with them. 'Bert kept ... kept saying her name over and over again, rocking her. And I touched his arm and tried to ... to let him know I was there. Just *there*, do you know? And he turned to me, but he didn't know who I was. He just turned to me and asked, "Claire?" As if he was asking me to deny it, to tell him that this ... this *dead* person he held in his arms wasn't his girl, do you know, Pete? Pete, do you know?' He began sobbing. 'Oh, that son of a bitch, that rotten son of a bitch.'

'Come on,' Byrnes said.

'Leave me alone.'

'Come on, Steve, I need you,' Byrnes said.

Carella was silent.

'I can't use you this way,' Byrnes said.

Carella sighed deeply. He pulled a handkerchief from his pocket and blew his nose. He put the handkerchief back into his pocket, his eyes avoiding Byrnes's, and he nodded and got off the stool, and then he sighed again.

'How ... how's Bert?' he asked.

'Meyer sent him home.'

Carella nodded.

'Did you question anybody?' Byrnes asked.

Carella shook his head.

'I think we ought to,' Byrnes said.

3

Byrnes was in the middle of signing his name to the report he had typed himself when the telephone rang. He lifted the receiver. '87th Squad, Byrnes here.'

'Pete, this is Hal. I'm still at the hospital.'

'Get anything?' Byrnes asked.

'The guy just died,' Willis said.

'Did he say anything?'

'Only one word, Pete. He repeated it several times.'

'What was the word?'

'Carpenter. He kept saying it, maybe four, five times before he died. Carpenter.'

'That's all he said?'

'That's all.'

'All right,' Byrnes said; 'see if they'll let you talk to the woman they have there. Name's Myra Klein. She's the one who fainted in the shop. They're treating her for shock.'

'Right,' Willis said, and he hung up.

Byrnes completed his signature.

Myra Klein was wearing a white hospital gown and complaining bitterly about the city's public servants when Willis came into her room. Apparently the police had sent Miss Klein off to the hospital against her wishes, and apparently she was being kept there now against her wishes. She swore at the nurse who was trying to administer a sedative, turned to the door as Willis opened it, and shouted, 'What do *you* want?'

'I'd like to—'

'Are you a doctor?'

'No, ma'am . . .'

'How do I get *out* of this madhouse?' Miss Klein shouted. 'Who are you?'

'Detective 3rd Grade Harold Will . . .'

24

'Detective?' Miss Klein shouted. 'Detective? Get him out of here!' she yelled at the nurse. 'You're the ones who *sent* me here!'

'No, ma'am, I just—'

'Is there a crime against passing out?'

'No, but—'

'I told them I was all right. I *told* them.'

'Well, ma'am, I—'

'Instead they stick me in an ambulance. Unconscious, when I can't defend myself.'

'But, ma'am, if you were unconscious, then how—'

'Don't tell *me* what I was,' Miss Klein shouted. 'I can take care of myself. I told them I was all right. They had no right sticking me in an ambulance, unconscious.'

'Who'd you tell, Mrs Klein?'

'It's *Miss* Klein – and what do you care who I told?'

'Well, Miss Klein, the point is—'

'Get him out of here. I don't want to talk to any cops.'

'—if you were unconscious—'

'I said get him out of here!'

'—how could you have possibly told anyone you were all right?'

Myra Klein stared at Willis in total silence for the space of two minutes. Then she said, 'What are you, one of these smart-assed cops?'

'Well—'

'I'm laying here prostrate in shock,' Miss Klein said, 'and they send me Sherlock Holmes.'

'Will you take this pill now, Miss Klein?' the nurse asked.

'Get out of here, you miserable panhandler, before I—'

'It'll calm you!' the nurse protested.

'Calm me? *Calm* me? What makes you think I need calming?'

'Leave the pill, nurse,' Willis said gently. 'Maybe Miss Klein will feel more like taking it later.'

'Yeah, leave the pill and get out, and take Mr Holmes with you.'

'No, I'm staying,' Willis said softly.

'Who sent for you? Who needs you?'

'I want to ask you some questions, Miss Klein,' Willis said.

'I don't want to answer any questions. I'm a sick woman. I'm in shock. Now get the hell out of here.'

'Miss Klein,' Willis said evenly, 'four people were killed.'

Myra Klein stared at him. Then she nodded her head. 'Leave the pill, nurse,' she said. 'I'll talk to Mr – what was your name?'

'Willis.'

'Yes. Leave the pill, nurse.' She waited until the door closed behind the nurse. Then she said, 'All I could think of was my brother's dinner. He gets home from work at seven o'clock, and it's past that now, and he's very fussy about his dinner being on the table when he gets home. So here I am laying in a hospital. That's all I could think of.' She paused. 'Then you said, "Four people were killed," and all at once I'm one of the lucky ones.' She nodded expressively. 'What do you want to know, Mr Willis?'

'Can you tell me what happened in that bookshop, Miss Klein?'

'Sure, I put on the roast about four-thirty – it's a shame to make roast when there's only myself and my brother, so much goes to waste, you know, but he likes roast beef, so every now and then I make it. I put it on at four-thirty – I have one of these automatic ranges, you can set it to go off when the thing is done. I had the potatoes on, too, and the string beans wouldn't take a minute once I got home. There was a book I wanted to get. They have a lending library at that bookstore, you see, over on the left – where I was standing when the man started shooting.'

'It was a man, Miss Klein?'

'Yes. I think so. I only got a quick look. I was standing at the place where Mr Fennerman has the lending library when all of a sudden I heard this loud noise. So I turned around, and I saw this man with two guns in his hands, shooting. At first, I didn't know what it was, I don't know what I thought – a stunt, I guess I thought – I don't know what. Then I saw a nice young man, he was wearing a seersucker suit, he suddenly collapsed on the counter, and he's covered all over with blood, and then I knew it wasn't a stunt, it couldn't be a stunt.'

'What happened then, Miss Klein?'

'I guess I passed out. I could never stand the sight of blood.'

'But you saw the man shooting before you passed out?'

'Yes, I did.'

'Can you tell me what he looked like?'

'Yes, I think so.' She paused. 'Where do you want me to start?'

'Well, was he a tall man? Short? Average height?'

'Average, I think.' She paused again. 'What do you mean by average?'

'Five-nine, five-ten.'

'Yes, about that.'

'He wasn't what you'd call a tall man?'

'No, I mean, he wasn't as short as . . .' She stopped.

'He wasn't as short as me?' Willis said, smiling.

'No. He was taller than you.'

'But not a really tall man. All right, Miss Klein, what was he wearing?'

'A raincoat,' Miss Klein said.

'What colour?'

'Black.'

'Belted or loose?'

'I didn't notice.'

'Any hat?'

'Yes.'

'What kind of hat?'

'A cap,' Miss Klein said.

'The colour?'

'Black. Like the raincoat.'

'Was he wearing gloves?'

'No.'

'Anything else you noticed about him?'

'Yes. He was wearing sunglasses.'

'From where you were standing, could you see any identifying scars or marks?'

'No.'

'Any deformities?'

'No.'

'Was this a white man or a coloured man, Miss Klein?'

'White.'

'Do you know anything about guns?'

'No.'

'Then you couldn't guess what kind of guns he was holding.'

'Kind?'

'Well, yes. The calibre, or whether they were revolvers or automatics or . . . well, were they small guns, Miss Klein?'

'They looked very big to me.'

'Do you know what a .45 looks like?'

'No, I'm sorry.'

'That's all right, Miss Klein; you're being very helpful. Can you tell me how old this man was?'

'About thirty-eight.'

'How old would you say I am, Miss Klein?'

'Thirty-six. Am I close?'

'I'll be thirty-four next month.'

'Well, that's pretty close.'

'Yes, you're a very observant witness, Miss Klein. I wonder if I could sum this up for us. You say you saw a white man of about thirty-eight, average height, and he was wearing a black raincoat, a black cap, and sunglasses. He wore no gloves, he was holding a big gun in each hand, and you noticed no scars or deformities. Is that about it?'

'That's it exactly,' Miss Klein said.

Now, obviously, Miss Klein's 'exactly' and Mr Fennerman's 'exactly' did not exactly add up to a picture of exactness. Willis had not yet read the report typed up by Lieutenant Byrnes and therefore had no way of knowing that the two descriptions of the same man – while agreeing on certain points – varied on a few essentials. For example, Mr Fennerman had said the killer was a tall man, perhaps six feet, perhaps more. Miss Klein, on the other hand, described the killer as being of average height, five-nine or five-ten. Fennerman had said that the killer was wearing a tweed overcoat and that the overcoat may have been blue. Miss Klein said he was wearing a black raincoat. Fennerman: grey fedora. Klein: black cap. Fennerman: black gloves. Klein: no gloves.

Willis knew nothing as yet of the discrepancies, but had he known he would not have been overly surprised. He had been questioning people about the details of committed crimes for a long time now and had discovered rather early in the game that most eyewitnesses had only the faintest notion of what had really taken place. Whatever the reason – the excitement of the moment, the speed of the action, the theory that participation blurred objectivity – whatever the reason an eye-witness description of any chosen event had a peculiar way of leaping into that rarefied atmosphere bordering on fantasy. He had heard the most bizarre contradictions during his years on the police force. He had heard housewives describing in total inaccuracy the clothing their husbands had worn when leaving the house that morning. He had heard pistols described as shotguns, razor blades described as knives, blondes described as brunettes, tall men as short men, fat men as thin men, and, in at least one case, a voluptuous eighteen-year-old red-headed girl described as a dark-haired man in his early twenties.

Willis still asked the questions because it was all part of the game. The game was something like parlour analysis, where the cops listened to each fantastic report and tried to piece together from the subjective dreamlike accounts a picture of objective reality. This picture was often impossible to obtain from the fragmentary distortions. Even when the criminal was finally apprehended, *his* account of the actual crime was tainted by the same subjective distortion. It made things a little difficult. It sometimes made a thoughtful cop like Willis wonder about the reality of a bullet-riddled body on a bookshop floor.

He thanked Miss Klein for her courtesy and her time and left her alone to take her pill and worry about her brother's dinner.

By the end of that day, Friday, October 13, all four survivors of the bookshop massacre had been questioned concerning the event itself and the identity of the killer. In the unaccustomed silence of the squad room, Detective Steve Carella sat down with the four typewritten reports and tried to make some sort of sensible correlation. He worked in pencil on the back of a D.D. report, listing first the names of the witnesses and then their descriptions of the killer. When he finished his list, he looked at it sourly, scratched his head, and then read it over again.

Fennerman	Klein	Deering	Woody
Male	Male	Male	Male
White	White	White	White
20–25	38	30	45
Tall	Average	Average	Tall
Overcoat, blue tweed	Raincoat, black	Overcoat, brown tweed	Overcoat, brown tweed
Grey fedora	Black cap	Grey fedora	Grey fedora
Sunglasses	Sunglasses	Sunglasses	Sunglasses
Black gloves	No gloves	Didn't notice	Gloves (not sure of colour)
No comment on	No scars, etc.	Scar on right cheek	No scars
Two guns	Two guns, big	One gun	Two guns .22 calibre

The witnesses seemed to agree wholeheartedly on only three points: the killer was male, and white, and wearing sunglasses. From their varying estimates of the man's age, Carella found it impossible to make an intelligent guess. Two of the witnesses thought the killer was tall, and two thought he was of average height – so Carella safely reasoned that, at least, the man was not short. Only one of the witnesses, Miss Klein, thought he was wearing a raincoat, whereas the other three agreed it was an overcoat. They could not get together on the colour of the coat, but two of them were certain it was brown. In any case, it was reasonable to assume the coat was dark. Carella was willing to buy the grey fedora since three of the four witnesses claimed this was what they had seen. The gloves were a toss-up. The scar seemed to have been invented by Miss Deering; two of the other witnesses said there had been no scars, and Mr Fennerman hadn't commented at all, a curious circumstance if there *had* been any scars. No, Carella was willing to rule out the possibility of the man's carrying a scar. Concerning the number of guns he'd carried, the majority of the witnesses seemed to agree it was two. Again, Miss Deering's imagination had taken hold, this time in understatement. Miss Klein said the guns were big, and Mr Woody – who himself owned a .22, for which he had a premises permit – claimed both guns were .22s.

Carella put a clean sheet of paper into his typewriter and began typing from his pencilled notes.

SUSPECT
Male
White
Not short

Sunglasses
Dark overcoat
Grey fedora
Gloves (?)
No scars, marks, deformities
Two guns

That was a lot to go on.
Sure.
That was a whole hell of a lot to go on.

'He could remember the day they met . . .

He was waiting in the hallway outside apartment 47, after having pressed the bell button. The door opened suddenly. He had heard no approaching footsteps, and the sudden opening of the door surprised him. Unconsciously, he looked first to the girl's feet. She was barefoot.

'My name is Bert Kling,' he said. 'I'm a cop.'

'You sound like the opening to a television show,' she answered.

She stared at Kling levelly. She was a tall girl. Even barefoot she reached to Kling's shoulder. In high heels she would give the average American male trouble. Her hair was black. Not brunette, not brownette, but black, a total black, the black of a starless, moonless night. Her eyes were a deep brown, arched with black brows. Her nose was straight and her cheeks were high, and there wasn't a trace of make-up on her face, not a tint of lipstick on her wide mouth. She wore a white blouse and black toreador pants, which tapered down to her naked ankles and feet. Her toenails were painted a bright red.

She kept staring at him. At last, she said, 'Why'd they send you here?'

'They said you knew Jeannie Paige.'

That was the beginning of Claire Townsend, or at least the beginning of her for him. He was still a patrolman at the time, and he had gone to her in plain clothes and on his own time to ask questions about a dead girl named Jeannie Paige, the sister-in-law of an old friend. She answered all his questions graciously and easily, and at last, when there were no more questions to ask, he rose and said, 'I'd better be going. That *is* dinner I smell, isn't it?'

'My father'll be home soon,' Claire said. 'Mom is dead. I whip something up when I get home from school.'

'Every night?' Kling asked.

'What? I'm sorry . . .'

He didn't know whether to press it or not. She hadn't heard him, and he could easily have shrugged his comment aside. But he chose not to.

'I said, "Every night?"'

'Every night what?'

She certainly was not making it easy for him. 'Do you prepare supper every night? Or do you occasionally get a night off?'

'Oh, I get nights off,' Claire said.

'Maybe you'd enjoy dinner out some night?'

'With you, do you mean?'

'Well, yes. Yes, that's what I had in mind.'

Claire Townsend looked at him long and hard. At last, she said, 'No, I don't think so. I'm sorry. Thanks. I couldn't.'

'Well . . . uh . . .' Quite suddenly, Kling felt like a horse's ass. 'I . . . uh . . . guess I'll be going then. Thanks for the cognac. It was very nice.'

'Yes,' she said, and he remembered her discussing people who were there and yet not there, and he knew exactly what she meant, because she was not there at all. She was somewhere far away, and he wished he knew where. With sudden, desperate longing, he wished he knew where she was because, curiously, he wanted to be there with her.

'Good-bye,' he said.

She smiled in answer and closed the door behind him . . .

He could remember.

He sat alone now in the furnished room that was his home. The windows were open. October lay just outside, alive with the sounds of the night-time city. He sat in a hard straight-backed chair and looked out past the curtains, gently stirring in a breeze far too mild for October. He looked beyond the curtains, and through the window, and into the city itself, into the lighted window slashes in the distance, and a klieg light going against the velvet sky, and an aeroplane blinking red and green, all the light of the city streets and the city buildings and the air above the city, all the lights, alive.

He could remember the SPRY sign . . .

Their first date was going badly. They had spent the afternoon together, and now they sat in a restaurant high atop one of the city's better-known hotels, and they looked through the huge windows which faced the river – and across the river there was a sign.

The sign first said: SPRY.

Then it said: SPRY FOR FRYING.

Then it said: SPRY FOR BAKING.

Then it said again: SPRY.

'What'll you drink?' Kling asked.

'A whisky sour, I think,' Claire said.

'No cognac?'

'Later maybe.'

The waiter came over to the table. 'Something to drink, sir?' he asked.

'A whisky sour and a Martini.'

'Lemon peel, sir?'

'Olive,' Kling said.

'Thank you, sir. Would you care to see a menu now?'

'We'll wait until after we've had our drinks, thank you. All right, Claire?'

'Yes, fine,' she said.

They sat in silence. Kling looked through the windows.

SPRY FOR FRYING.

'Claire?'

'Yes?'

SPRY FOR BAKING.

'It's been a bust, hasn't it?'

'Please, Bert.'

'The rain ... and that lousy movie. I didn't want it to be this way. I wanted—'

'I knew this would happen, Bert. I tried to tell you, didn't I? Didn't I try to warn you off? Didn't I tell you I was the dullest girl in the world? Why did you insist, Bert? Now you make me feel like a ... like a—'

'I don't want you to feel *any* way,' he said. 'I was only going to suggest that we ... we start afresh. From now. Forgetting everything that's ... that's happened.'

'Oh, what's the use?'

'Claire,' he said evenly, 'what the hell's the matter with you?'

'Nothing.'

'Where do you go when you retreat?'

'What?'

'Where do you—'

'I didn't think it showed. I'm sorry.'

'It shows,' Kling said. 'Who was he?'

Claire looked up sharply. 'You're a better detective than I realized.'

'It doesn't take much detection,' he said. There was a sad undertone to his voice, as if her confirmation of his suspicions had suddenly taken all the fight out of him. 'I don't mind your carrying a torch. Lots of girls—'

'It's not that,' she interrupted.

'Lots of girls do,' he continued. 'A guy drops them cold, or else it just peters out the way romances sometimes—'

'It's not that!' she said sharply, and when he looked across the table at her, her eyes were filmed with tears.

'Hey, listen, I—'

'Please, Bert, I don't want to—'

'But you said it *was* a guy. You said—'

'All right,' she answered. 'All right, Bert.' She bit down on her lip. 'All right, there was a guy. And I was in love with him. I was seventeen – just like Jeannie Paige – and he was nineteen. We hit it off right away ... do you know how such things happen, Bert? It happened that way with us. We made a lot of plans, big plans. We were young, and we were strong, and we were in love.'

'I ... I don't understand,' he said.

'He was killed in Korea.'

Across the river, the sign blared: SPRY FOR FRYING.

The tears. The bitter tears, starting slowly at first, forcing their way past clenched eyelids, trickling silently down her cheeks. Her shoulders began to heave, and she sat as still as a stone, her hands clasped in her lap, her shoulders heaving, sobbing silently while the tears coursed down her face. He had never seen such honest misery before. He turned his face away. He did not want to watch her. She sobbed steadily for several moments, and then the tears stopped as suddenly as they had begun, leaving her face looking as clean as a city street after a sudden summer storm.

'I'm sorry,' she said.

'Don't be.'

'I should have cried a long time ago.'

'Yes.'

The waiter brought the drinks. Kling lifted his glass. 'To a new beginning,' he said.

Claire studied him. It took her a long time to reach for the drink before her. Finally her hand closed around the glass. She lifted it and touched the rim of Kling's glass. 'To a new beginning,' she said. She threw off the drink quickly.

She looked across at him as if she were seeing him for the first time. The tears had put a sparkle into her eyes. 'It ... it may take time, Bert,' she said. Her voice came from a long way off.

'I've got all the time in the world,' he said. And then, almost afraid she would laugh at him, he added, 'All I've been doing is killing time, Claire, waiting for you to come along.'

She seemed ready to cry again. He reached across the table and covered her hand with his. 'You're ... you're very good, Bert,' she said, her voice growing thin, the way a voice does before it collapses into tears. 'You're good, and kind, and gentle, and you're quite beautiful, do you know that? I ... I think you're very beautiful.'

'You should see me when my hair is combed,' he said, smiling, squeezing her hand.

'I'm not joking,' she said. 'You always think I'm joking, and you really shouldn't, because I'm ... I'm a serious girl.'

'I know.'

'Bert,' she said. 'Bert.' And she put her other hand over his, so that three hands formed a pyramid on the table. Her face grew very serious. 'Thank you, Bert. Thank you so very, very much.'

He didn't know what to say. He felt embarrassed and stupid and happy and very big. He felt about eighty feet tall.

She leaned forward suddenly and kissed him, a quick sudden kiss that fleetingly touched his mouth and then was gone. She sat back again, seeming very unsure of herself, seeming like a frightened little girl at her first party. 'You ... you must be patient,' she said.

'I will,' he promised.

The waiter suddenly appeared. The waiter was smiling. He coughed discreetly. 'I thought,' he said gently, 'perhaps a little candlelight at the table, sir? The lady will look even more lovely by candlelight.'

'The lady looks lovely just as she is,' Kling said.

The waiter seemed disappointed. 'But ...'

'But the candlelight, certainly,' Kling said. 'By all means, the candlelight.'

The waiter beamed. 'Ah, yes, sir. Yes, sir. And then we will order, yes? I have some suggestions, sir, whenever you're ready.' He paused, his smile lighting his face. 'It's a beautiful night, sir, isn't it?'

'It's a wonderful night,' Claire answered ...

Alone in the night, alone in the light-blinking silence of his furnished room, he tried to tell himself she was not dead. He had spoken to her this afternoon. She had told him about her new bra. She was not dead. She was still alive and vibrant. She was still Claire Townsend.

She was dead.

He sat staring through the window.

He felt numb and cold. There was no feeling in his hands. If he moved his fingers, he knew they would not respond. He sat heavily, shivering in the warm October breeze, staring through the window at the myriad lights of the city, how gently the curtain rustled in the caressing wind, he felt nothing but an empty coldness, something hard and rigid and frighteningly cold at the pit of his stomach, he could not move, he could not cry, he could not feel.

She was dead.

No, he told himself, and he allowed a faint smile to turn the corners of his mouth; no, don't be ridiculous. Claire dead? Don't be ridiculous. I spoke to her this afternoon. She called me at the squad room, the way she always calls. Meyer was making jokes about it. Carella was there – he could tell you. He remembers. She called me, and they were both there, so I know I wasn't dreaming, and if she called me she must be alive, isn't that so? That's only logical. She called me, so I know she's alive. Carella was there. Ask Carella. He'll tell you. He'll tell you Claire is alive.

He could remember talking to Carella once not too long ago in a diner, the plate-glass window splashed with rain. There had been an intimacy to the place, a rained-in snugness as they had discussed the case they were working, as they had lifted steaming coffee mugs. And into the intimate mood of the moment, into the rain-protected comfort of the room, Carella had said, 'When are you going to marry that girl?'

'She wants to get her master's degree before we get married,' Kling said.

'Why?'

'How do I know? She's insecure. She's psychotic. How do I know?'

'What does she want after the master's? A doctorate?'

'Maybe.' Kling had shrugged. 'Listen, I ask her to marry me every time I see her. She wants the master's. So what can I do? I'm in love with her. Can I tell her to go to hell?'

'I suppose not.'

'Well, I can't.' Kling had paused. 'You want to know something, Steve?'

'What?'

'I wish I could keep my hands off her. You know, I wish we didn't have to ... well, you know, my landlady looks at me cockeyed every time I bring Claire upstairs. And then I have to rush her home because her father is the strictest guy who ever walked the earth. I'm surprised he's leaving her alone this weekend. But what I mean is ... well, damn it, what the hell does she need that master's for, Steve? I mean, I wish I could leave her alone until we were married, but I just can't. I mean, all I have to do is to be with her, and my mouth goes dry. Is it that way with ... well, never mind, I didn't mean to get personal.'

'It's that way,' Carella had said.

She's alive, Kling reasoned.

Of course, she's alive. She's going for her master's degree. She's already doing social field work. Why, just today, on the telephone, she told me she'd be a little late: *I have to pick up some texts.*

Interviewing: Its Principles and Methods, he thought.

Patterns of Culture, he thought.

The Sane Society, he thought.

She's dead, he thought.

'NO!'

He screamed the word aloud into the silence of the room. The scream brought him physically out of the chair, as if the force of its explosion had lifted him.

'*No*,' he said again, very softly, and he walked to the window, and he rested his head against the curtain, and he looked down into the street, looking for Claire. She should have been here by now. It was almost ... what time was it? What time? He knew her walk. He would recognize her the moment she turned into the block – a white blouse, she had said; that and a black skirt – yes, he would know her instantly. He wondered abruptly what the bra looked like, and again he smiled, the curtain soft and reassuring against his cheek, the lights of the restaurant across the way staining his face in alternating red and green neon.

I wonder what's keeping her, he thought.

Well, she's dead, you know, he thought.

He turned away from the window. He walked to the bed, and he looked at it unseeingly, and then he walked to the dresser, and he stared down at its cluttered top, and picked up the hairbrush, and saw strands of her black hair tangled in its bristles, and put down the brush, and looked at his watch, and did not see the time.

It was almost midnight.

He walked back to the window and stared down into the street again, waiting for her.

By six a.m. the next morning he knew she was not coming.

He knew he would never see her again.

5

A police precinct is a small community within a community. There were one hundred and eighty-six patrolmen attached to the precinct and sixteen detectives attached to the squad. The men of the precinct and the squad knew each other the way people in a small town do: there were close friendships, and nodding acquaintanceships, and minor feuds, and strictly formal business relationships. But all of the men who used the station house as their office knew each other by sight, and usually by name, even if they had never worked a case together.

By seven forty-five the next morning, when a third of the precinct patrolmen were relieved on post, when the three detectives upstairs were officially relieved, there was not a single man in the precinct – uniformed or plainclothes – who did not know that Bert Kling's girl had been killed in a bookstore on Culver Avenue.

Most of the cops didn't even know her name. To them, she was a vague image, real nonetheless, a person somewhat like their own wives or sweethearts, a young girl who took on personality, who became flesh and blood only by association with their own loved ones. She was Bert Kling's girl, and she was dead.

'Kling?' some of the patrolmen asked. 'Which one is he?'

'Kling's girl?' some of the detectives asked. 'You're kidding! You mean it?'

'Man, that's a lousy break,' some of them said.

A police precinct is a small community within a community.

The cops of the 87th Precinct – uniformed and plainclothes – understood that Kling was one of them. There were men among the patrolmen who knew him only as the blond bull who had answered a squeal while they were keeping a timetable. If they'd met him in an official capacity, they would have called him 'sir'. There were other men who had been patrolmen when Kling was still walking a beat, and who were still patrolmen, and who resented his promotion somewhat because he seemed to be just a lucky stiff who'd happened to crack a murder case. There were detectives who felt Kling would have made a better shoe clerk than a detective. There were detectives who felt Kling was indispensable on a case, combining a mature directness with a boyish humility, a combination which could pry answers from the most stubborn witness. There were stool pigeons who felt Kling was tight with a buck. There were prostitutes on *La Via de Putas* who eyed Kling secretly and who admitted among themselves that for this particular cop they wouldn't mind throwing away a free one. There were shop owners who felt he was too strict about city ordinances concerning sidewalk stands. There were kids in the precinct who knew that Kling would look the other way if they turned on a fire hydrant during the summer. There were other kids in the precinct who knew that Kling would break their hands if he caught them fiddling with narcotics, even with something as harmless as mootah. There were traffic cops who called him

'Blondie' behind his back. There was one detective on the squad who hated to read any of Kling's reports because he was a lousy typist and a worse speller. Miscolo, in the Clerical Office, had a suspicion that Kling didn't like the coffee he made.

But all of the cops of the 87th, and many of the citizens who lived in the precinct territory, understood that Kling was one of them.

Oh, there was none of that condolence-card sentiment about their understanding, none of that 'your loss is my loss' horse manure. Actually, Kling's loss was not their loss, and they knew it. Claire Townsend was only a name to most of them, and not even that much to some of them. But Kling was a policeman. Every other cop in the precinct knew that he was a part of the club, and you didn't go around hurting club members or the people they loved.

And so, whereas none of them agreed to it, whereas all of them discussed the crime but none of them discussed what he personally was going to do about it, a curious thing happened on October 14. On October 14 every cop in the precinct stopped being a cop. Well, he didn't turn in his badge and his service revolver – nothing as dramatic as that. But being a cop in the 87th meant being a lot of things, and it meant being them *all* of the time. On October 14 the cops of the 87th still went about their work, which happened to be crime prevention, and they went about it in much the same way as always. Except for one difference.

They arrested muggers, and pushers, and con men, and rapists, and drunks, and junkies, and prostitutes. They discouraged loitering and betting on the horses and unlawful assembly and crashing red lights and gang warfare. They rescued cats and babies and women with their heels caught in grates. They helped schoolchildren across the street. They did everything just the way they always did it. Except for the difference.

The difference was this: their ordinary daily chores, the things they did every day of the week – their *work* – became a hobby. Or an avocation. Or call it what you will. They were doing it, and perhaps they did it well, but under the guise of working at all the petty little infractions that bugged cops everywhere, they were *really* working on the Kling Case. They didn't call it The Bookstore Case, or The Claire Townsend Case, or The Massacre Case, or anything of the sort. It was The Kling Case. From the moment their day started to the moment their day ended, they were actively at work on it, listening, watching, waiting. Although only four men were officially assigned to the case, the man who'd done that bookshop killing had two hundred and two policemen looking for him.

Steve Carella was one of those policemen.

He had gone home at midnight the night before. At two o'clock, unable to sleep, he had called Kling.

'Bert?' he had said. 'How are you?'

'I'm fine,' Kling had answered.

'Did I wake you?'

'No,' Kling had said. 'I was up.'

'What were you doing, kid?'

'Watching. Watching the street.'

They had talked a while longer, and then Carella had said good-bye and hung up. He had not fallen asleep until four o'clock that morning. The image of Kling in his room, alone, watching the street, had kept drifting in and out of his dreams. At eight o'clock he had awakened, dressed and driven down to the squad room.

Meyer Meyer was already there.

'I want to try something on you, Steve,' Meyer said.

'Go ahead.'

'Do you buy this guy as a fanatic?'

'No,' Carella said immediately.

'Me, neither. I've been up all night, thinking about what happened in that bookstore. I couldn't sleep a wink.'

'I didn't sleep well either,' Carella said.

'I figured if the guy is a fanatic, he's going to do the same thing tomorrow, right? He'll walk into a supermarket tomorrow and he'll shoot four more people at random, am I right?'

'That's right,' Carella said.

'But that's only if he's a lunatic. And it sounds like a madman, doesn't it? The guy walks into a store and starts blasting? He's got to be nuts, right?' Meyer nodded. 'But I don't buy it.'

'Why not?'

'Instinct. Intuition. I don't know why. I just know this guy is not a madman. I think he wanted somebody in that store dead. I think he knew his victim was going to be in that store, and I think he walked in and began blasting and didn't give a damn who else he killed, so long as he killed the person he was after. That's what I think.'

'That's what I think, too,' Carella said.

'Good. So, assuming he got who he was after, I think we ought to—'

'Suppose he didn't, Meyer?'

'Didn't what?'

'Get who he was after.'

'I thought of that, too, Steve, but I ruled it out. It suddenly came to me in the middle of the night – Jesus, suppose he was after one of the survivors? We'd better get police protection to them right away. But then I ruled it out.'

'I did, too,' Carella said.

'How do you figure?'

'There were three areas in that shop,' Carella said. 'The two aisles, and the high counter where Fennerman was sitting. If our killer wanted Fennerman, he'd have shot directly at him, at the counter. If he'd wanted somebody in the far aisles, where the other three survivors were standing, he'd have blasted in that direction. But, instead, he walked into the shop and began shooting immediately into the nearest aisle. The way I figure it, his victim is dead, Meyer. He *got* who he was after.'

'There're a few other things to consider, Steve,' Meyer said.

'What?'

'We don't know who he was after, so we'll have to start asking questions. But remember, Steve . . .'

'I know.'

'What?'

'Claire Townsend was killed.'

Meyer nodded. 'There's a possibility,' he said, 'that *Claire* was the one he was gunning for.'

*

The man in the seersucker suit was named Herbert Land.

He taught philosophy at the university on the fringes of the precinct territory. He often went to The Browser because it was close to the school and he could pick up secondhand *Plato* and *Descartes* there at reasonable prices. The man in the seersucker suit was dead because he had been standing in the aisle closest to the door when the killer had cut loose with his barrage.

Herbert Land .... DOA

Land had lived in a development house in the nearby suburb of Sands Spit. He had lived there with his wife and two children. The oldest of the kids was six. The youngest was three. Herbert Land's widow, a woman named Veronica, was twenty-eight years old. The moment Meyer and Carella saw her standing in the doorway of the development house they realized she was pregnant. She was a plain woman with brown hair and blue eyes, but she stood in the doorway with a quiet dignity that belied the tear-streaked face and the red-rimmed eyes. She stood and asked them quietly who they were, and then asked to see their identification, standing in the classic posture of the pregnant woman, her belly extended, one hand resting almost on the small of her back, her head slightly tilted. They showed their shields and their ID cards, and she nodded briefly and allowed them to enter her home.

The house was very still. Veronica Land explained that her mother had come to take the children away for a few days. The children did not yet know their father had been killed. She would have to tell them, she knew, but she wanted to be composed when she did, and she had not yet adjusted to the fact herself. She spoke in a low, controlled voice, but the tears sat just behind her eyes, waiting to be released, and the detectives picked through the conversation delicately and cautiously, not wanting to release the torrent. She sat very stiffly in an easy chair, carrying her unborn child like a huge medicine ball in her lap. She did not take her eyes from the detectives as they spoke. Carella had the feeling that every shred of her being was furiously concentrated on what they were saying. He had the feeling that she was clinging to the conversation for support, that if she once lost its thread she would burst into uncontrollable tears.

'How old was your husband, Mrs Land?' Meyer asked.

'Thirty-one.'

'And he was a teacher at the university, is that right?'

'An instructor, yes. As assistant professor.'

'He commuted daily from Sands Spit?'

'Yes.'

'What time did he leave the house, Mrs Land?'

'He caught the eight-seventeen each morning.'

'Do you own a car, Mrs Land?'

'Yes.'

'But your husband took the train?'

'Yes. We have only one car, and I'm ... well, as you can see, I'm going to have a baby. Herbie ... Herbie felt I should have the car here. In case ... well ...'

'When is the baby due, Mrs Land?' Carella asked.

'It's supposed to come this month,' she answered. 'Sometime this month.'

Carella nodded. The house went still again.

Meyer cleared his throat. 'What time does the eight-seventeen reach the city, would you know, Mrs Land?'

'Nine o'clock, I think. I know his first class was at nine-thirty, and he had to take a subway uptown from the terminal. I think the train got in at nine, yes.'

'And he taught philosophy?'

'He was in the philosophy department, yes. Actually he taught philosophy and ethics and logic and aesthetics.'

'I see. Mrs Land ... did ... uh ... did your husband seem worried about anything? Did he mention anything that might have seemed ...'

'Worried? What do you mean, worried?' Veronica Land said. 'He was worried about his salary, which is six thousand dollars a year, and he was worried about our mortgage payments, and worried about the one car we have which is about to fall apart. What do you mean "worried"? I don't know what you mean by "worried".'

Meyer glanced at Carella. For a moment the tension in the

room was unbearable. Veronica Land fought for control, clasped her hands in her lap just below the bulge of her stomach. She sighed heavily.

In a very low voice she said, 'I'm sorry, I don't know what you mean by "worried",' but she had regained control, and the edge of hysteria was gone now. 'I'm sorry.'

'Well, did . . . did he have any enemies that you know of?'

'None.'

'Any instructors at the university with whom he may have . . . well . . . argued . . . or . . . well, I don't know. Any departmental difficulties?'

'No.'

'Had anyone threatened him?'

'No.'

'His students perhaps? Had he talked about any difficulties with students? Had he failed anyone who might possibly have—'

'No.'

'—carried a grudge against—'

'Wait, yes.'

'What?' Carella said.

'Yes, he failed someone. But that was last semester.'

'Who?' Carella asked.

'A boy in his logic class.'

'Do you know his name?'

'Yes. Barney . . . something. Just a minute. He was on the baseball team, and when Herbie failed him he wasn't allowed to . . . Robinson, that was it. Barney Robinson.'

'Barney Robinson,' Carella repeated. 'And you say he was on the baseball team?'

'Yes. They play in the spring semester, you know. That was when Herbie failed him. Last semester.'

'I see. Do you know why he failed him, Mrs Land?'

'Why, yes. He . . . he wasn't doing his work. Why else would Herbie have failed him?'

'And because he failed he wasn't allowed to play on the team, is that right?'

'That's right.'

'Did your husband seem to think Robinson was carrying any resentment?'

'I don't know. You asked me if I could think of someone, and I just thought of this Robinson because ... Herbie didn't *have* any enemies, Mr – what was your name?'

'Carella.'

'Mr Carella, Herbie didn't have any enemies. You didn't know my husband so ... so ... you wouldn't know what ... what kind of a person he ...'

She was about to lose control again. Quickly Carella said, 'Did you ever meet this Robinson?'

'No.'

'Then you wouldn't know whether he was tall or short or—'

'No.'

'I see. And your husband discussed him with you, is that right?'

'He only told me he'd had to fail Barney Robinson, and that it meant the boy wouldn't be able to ... pitch, I think it was.'

'He's a pitcher, is that right?'

'Yes,' she paused. 'I think so. Yes. A pitcher.'

'That's a very important person on a team, Mrs Land. The pitcher.'

'Is he?'

'Yes. So there's the possibility that, in addition to Robinson himself, any number of students could have been resentful of your husband's actions. Isn't that so?'

'I don't know. He never mentioned it except that once.'

'Did any of his colleagues ever mention it?'

'Not that I know of.'

'Did you know any of his colleagues socially?'

'Yes, of course.'

'But they never mentioned Barney Robinson or the fact that your husband had failed him?'

'Never.'

'Not even jokingly?'

'Not at all.'

'Had your husband ever received any threatening letters, Mrs Land?'

'No.'

'Calls?'

'No.'

'But yet you thought of Robinson instantly when we asked if anyone might have a grudge against your husband.'

'Yes. I think it troubled Herbie. Having to fail him, I mean.'

'Did he *say* it troubled him?'

'No. But I know my own husband. He wouldn't have mentioned it if it wasn't troubling him.'

'But he told you about it *after* he'd failed the boy?'

'Yes.'

'How old is Robinson, do you know?'

'I don't know.'

'Do you have any idea what class he was in?'

'What do you mean?'

'Well, would he have graduated already? Or is he still at the school?'

'I don't know.'

'All you know, then, is that your husband failed a boy named Barney Robinson, a baseball player in his logic class.'

'Yes, that's all I know,' Veronica said.

'Thank you very much, Mrs Land. We appreciate—'

'And I know my husband is dead,' Veronica Land said tonelessly. 'I know that, too.'

The university buildings rose in scholastic splendour in the midst of squalor, a tribute to the vagaries of city development. Those many years back, when the university was planned and executed, the surrounding neighbourhood was one of the best in the city, containing several small parks, and rows of dignified brownstones, and apartment buildings with doormen. A slum grows because it has to have some place to go. In this case, it grew towards the university, and around the university, ringing it with poverty and contained hostility. The university remained an island of culture and learning, its green grass providing a moat which defied further encroachment. Student and professor alike came out of the subway each morning and walked book-laden through a neighbourhood where *The Razor's Edge* was not a novel by Somerset Maugham but a fact of life. Oddly, there were few incidents between the people of the neighbourhood and the university people. Once a student was mugged on his way to the subway, and once a young girl was almost raped, but a sort of undeclared truce existed, a *laissez faire* attitude which enabled citizen and scholar to pursue separate lives with a minimum of interference.

One of those scholars was Barney Robinson.

They found him on a campus bench, talking to a young brunette who had escaped from a Kerouac novel. They explained who they were and the girl excused herself. Robinson didn't seem particularly pleased by the intrusion, or by the girl's sudden disappearance.

'What's this all about?' he asked. He had blue eyes and a square face, and he was wearing a sweat shirt emblazoned with the name of the university. He straddled the bench and squinted into the sun, looking up at Meyer and Carella.

'We didn't expect to find you here today,' Carella said. 'Do you always have classes on Saturday?'

'What? Oh, no. Practice.'

'What do you mean?'

'Basketball.'

'We thought you were on the baseball team.'

'I am. I'm also on the basket ...' Robinson paused. 'How'd you know that? What is this?'

'Anyway, we're glad we caught you,' Carella said.

'*Caught* me?'

'That's just an expression.'

'Yeah, I hope so,' Robinson said glumly.

'How tall are you, Mr Robinson?' Meyer asked.

'Six-two.'

'How old are you?'

'Twenty-five.'

'Mr Robinson, did you once take a class with Professor Land?'

'Yeah.' Robinson kept squinting up at the detectives, trying to understand what they were driving at. His tone was cautious but not overly wary. He seemed only to be extremely puzzled.

'When was this?'

'Last semester.'

'What was the class?'

'Logic.'

'How'd you make out?'

'I flunked.'

'Why?'

Robinson shrugged.

'Do you think you deserved to flunk?'

Robinson shrugged again.

'Well, what do you say?' Meyer asked.

'I don't know. I flunked, that's all.'

'Were you doing the work?'

'Sure I was doing the work.'

'Did you understand what you were doing?'

'Yeah, I thought so,' Robinson said.

'But you flunked anyway.'

'Yeah.'

'Well, how'd you feel about that?' Meyer asked. 'You were doing the work, and you say you understood it, but still you flunked. How about that? How'd it make you feel?'

'Lousy – how do you think?' Robinson said. 'Would you mind telling me what this is all about? Since when do detectives—'

'This is just a routine investigation,' Carella said.

'Into what?' Robinson asked.

'How'd you feel about flunking?'

'I told you. Lousy. An investigation into what?'

'Well, that's not important, Mr Robinson. The only—'

'What is it? Is there a fix in or something?'

'A fix?'

'Yeah. The team, is that it? Is somebody trying to fix a game?'

'Why? Have you been approached?'

'Hell, no. If there's something going on, I don't know anything about it.'

'Are you a good basketball player, Mr Robinson?'

'Fair. Baseball's my game.'

'You pitch, is that right?'

'Yeah, that's right. You know an awful lot about me, don't you? For a routine investigation—'

'Are you a good pitcher?'

'Yes,' Robinson answered without hesitation.

'What happened when Land flunked you?'

'I got benched.'

'For how long?'

'For the rest of the season.'

'How'd this affect the team?'

Robinson shrugged. 'I don't want to blow my own horn . . .'

'Go ahead,' Meyer said, 'blow it.'

'We lost eight out of twelve.'

'Think you'd have won them if you were pitching?'

'Let's put it this way,' Robinson said. 'I think we'd have won *some* of them.'

'But, instead, you lost.'

'Yeah.'

'How'd the team feel about this?'

'Lousy. We thought we might cop the city championship. We were unbeaten until I was benched. Then we lost those eight games and we wound up in second place.'

'Well, that's not so bad,' Carella said.

'There's only one first place,' Robinson answered.

'Did the team feel Mr Land had been unfair?'

'I don't know how they felt.'

'How'd *you* feel?'

'Look, those are the breaks,' Robinson said.

'Yes, but how'd you feel?'

'I thought I knew the work.'

'Then why'd he flunk you?'

'Why don't you go ask him?' Robinson said.

This was the place to say 'Because he's dead,' but neither Meyer nor Carella said the words. They watched Robinson squinting up into their faces and into the sun, and Carella said, 'Where were you last night about five o'clock, Mr Robinson?'

'Why?'

'We'd like to know.'

'I don't think that's any of your business,' Robinson said.

'I'm afraid we'll have to be the judge of what's our business or what isn't.'

'Then maybe you better go get a warrant for my arrest,' Robinson said. 'If this is as serious as all that—'

'Nobody said it was serious, Mr Robinson.'

'No?'

'No.' Meyer paused. 'Do you want us to get that warrant?'

'I don't see why I have to tell you—'

'It might help us to clear up a few things, Mr Robinson.'

'What things?'

'Where were you last night at five o'clock?'

'I was ... I was involved in something personal.'

'Like what?'

'Look, I don't see any reason—'

'What were you involved in?'

'I was with a girl,' Robinson said, sighing.

'From what time to what time?'

'From about four ... well, a little before four ... my last class broke at three forty-five ...'

'Yes, from three forty-five until when?'

'Until about eight.'

'Where were you?'

'At the girl's apartment.'

'Where?'

'Downtown.'

'Where downtown?'

'For Christ's sake ...'

'Where?'

'On Tremayne Avenue. It's in the Quarter, near Canopy.'

'You were at the apartment at four o'clock?'

'No, we must've got there about four-fifteen, four-thirty.'

'But you *were* there at five?'

'Yes.'

'What were you doing?'

'Well, you know ...'

'Tell us.'

'I don't *have* to tell you! You figure it out for yourself, goddamn it!'

'OK. What's the girl's name?'

'Olga.'

'Olga what?'

'Olga Wittensten.'

'Was that the girl just sitting here with you?'

'Yeah. What're you gonna do – question her, too? You gonna foul up a good thing?'

'All we want to do is check your story, Mr Robinson. The rest is your problem.'

'This is a very high-strung girl,' Robinson said. 'She's liable to spook. I don't understand what this is all about anyway. Why do you have to check my story? What is it I'm supposed to have done?'

'You're supposed to have been in an apartment on Tremayne Avenue from four-fifteen yesterday afternoon to eight o'clock last night. If you were doing what you're supposed to have been doing, you'll never see us again as long as you live, Mr Robinson.'

'Well, maybe not as long as you live,' Meyer amended.

'Which means you'll be back Monday morning,' Robinson said.

'Why? *Weren't* you in that apartment?'

'I was there, I was there. Go on and check. But the last time there was a basketball scandal, we had detectives and district attorneys and special investigators crawling all over the campus for weeks. If this is the same thing—'

'This isn't the same thing, Mr Robinson.'

'I hope not. I'm clean. I play a clean game. I never took a nickel, and I never will. You just remember that.'

'We will.'

'And when you talk to Olga, for Pete's sake, try not to foul this up, will you? Will you please do me that favour? She's a very high-strung girl.'

They found Olga Wittensten in the student cafeteria drinking a cup of black coffee. She said like man, she had never before seen fuzz up close like this. She said yeah, she had a pad on Tremayne, downtown in the Quarter. She said she like waited for Barney yesterday afternoon, and they cut out to her place

53

and got there about four, four-thirty, something like that. She said they were there all afternoon, like maybe till eight o'clock or so, when they went out to break some bread. Like what was this all about?

Like it was about murder.

6

Bert Kling arrived at the squad room at two o'clock that Saturday afternoon, in time to see the report which had been delivered from Ballistics downtown. He was unshaven, a blond bristle covering his jowls and his chin. He was wearing the same suit and shirt he'd worn the night before, but he had taken off his tie, and his clothes looked as if he'd worn them to sleep. He accepted a few condolences in the corridor outside the squad room, turned down the coffee Miscolo offered him, and went directly into the lieutenant's office. He stayed with Byrnes for a half hour. When he came out into the squad room again, Carella and Meyer had returned from the university, where a promising lead had turned as dead as ashes. He went to Carella's desk.

'Steve,' he said. 'I'm working on it.'

Carella looked up and nodded. 'Think that's a good idea?'

'I just spoke to the lieutenant,' Kling said. His voice was curiously toneless. 'He thinks it'll be all right.'

'I just thought—'

'I want to work on it, Steve.'

'All right.'

'Actually, I . . . I was here when the squeal came in, so . . . so officially I . . .'

'It's all right with me, Bert. I was only thinking of you.'

'I'll be all right when we find him,' Kling said.

Carella and Meyer exchanged a silent glance.

54

'Well ... well, then, sure. Sure. You ... you want to see this Ballistics report?'

Kling took the Manila envelope silently, and silently he opened it. There were two reports in the envelope. One described a .45-calibre automatic. The other described a .22. Kling studied each of the reports separately.

There is nothing very mysterious about determining the make of an unknown firearm when one possesses a sample bullet fired from it. Kling, as a working cop, knew this. At the same time, he found the process a little confusing, and he tried not to think about it too much or too often.

He knew that there was a vast working file of revolvers, pistols, and bullets in the Ballistics Bureau, and that all these were classified by calibre, by number of lands and grooves, and by direction of the rifling twist. In addition, he knew that all hand guns in current use had rifled bores which put a fired bullet in rotation as it passed through the barrel. Lands, he had learned by rote, were the smooth surfaces between the spiral grooves in the barrel. Lands and grooves left marks upon a bullet.

When a spent bullet was recovered and sent to Ballistics, it was rolled on a sheet of carbon paper and then compared against the specimen cards in the file. If Ballistics tentatively made a bullet from the file cards, the suspect bullet was put under a microscope with a test bullet from another part of the file and both were accurately compared. Along about then, when twist and angle of twist entered the picture, Kling got a little confused.

That's why he never thought much about it. He knew simply that the same make of pistol or revolver would *always* fire a bullet with the same number and width of grooves and the same spiral direction and twist. So he accepted the Ballistics reports unquestioningly.

'He used two different guns, huh?' Kling said.

'Yes,' Carella answered. 'That explains the conflicting reports from our eyewitnesses. You didn't see those, Bert. They're in the file.'

'Under what?'

'Under . . .' Carella hesitated. 'Under K . . . for Kling.'

Kling nodded briefly. It was difficult to tell what he was thinking in that moment.

'We figured he was after one of the four he got, Bert,' Meyer said. He spoke cautiously and slowly. One of the four had been Claire Townsend.

Kling nodded.

'We don't know which one,' Carella said.

'We questioned Mrs Land this morning, and she gave us what looked like a lead, but it fizzled. We want to hit the others today and tomorrow.'

'I'll take one,' Kling said. He paused. 'I'd rather not question Claire's father, but any of the others . . .'

'Sure,' Carella said.

The men were silent. Both Meyer and Carella knew that something had to be said, and it had to be said now. Meyer was the senior of the two men – in age and in years with the squad – but he looked to Carella pleadingly, and Carella took the cue, cleared his throat, and said, 'Bert, I think . . . I think we ought to get something straight.'

Kling looked up.

'We want this guy. We want him very bad.'

'I know that.'

'We've got almost nothing to go on, and that doesn't make it easy. It'll make it harder if—'

'If *what*?'

'If we don't work this as a team.'

'We're working as a team,' Kling said.

'Bert, are you sure you want in on this?'

'I'm sure.'

'Are you sure you can question somebody and listen to the facts of Claire's death and be able to think of—'

'I can do it,' Kling said immediately.

'Don't cut me off, Bert. I'm talking about a multiple murder in a bookstore, and one of the victims was—'

'I said I can do it.'

'—one of the victims was Claire Townsend. Now can you?'

'Don't be a son of a bitch, Steve. I can do it, and I want to do it, and—'

'I don't think so.'

'Well *I* think so!' Kling said heatedly.

'You won't even let me mention her name here in the squad room, for Christ's sake! What are you going to do when someone describes the way she was killed?'

'I know she was killed,' Kling said softly.

'Bert . . .'

'I know she's dead.'

'Look, stay off it. Do me a favour and—'

'Friday the thirteenth,' Kling said. 'My mother used to call it a hoodoo jinx of a day. I know she's dead, Steve. I'll be able to . . . to . . . I'll work with you, and I'll be thinking straight, don't worry. You don't know how much I want to catch this guy. You just don't know how much I won't be good for anything else until we get him, believe me. I won't be good for another goddamn thing.'

'There's the possibility,' Carella said evenly, 'that the killer was after Claire.'

'I know.'

'There's the possibility we may find out things about Claire you wouldn't particularly like to know.'

'There's nothing new I can find out about Claire.'

'Homicide opens a lot of closets, Bert.'

'Where do you want me to go?' Kling asked. 'What do you want me to do?'

Carella and Meyer exchanged another long glance. 'OK,' Carella said at last. 'Go home and shave and change your clothes. Here's the address of Mrs Joseph Wechsler. We're trying to find out if any of the victims had any warnings or threats or . . . we want to find out exactly *who* he was after, Bert.'

'All right.' Kling picked up the sheet of paper, folded it in two, and slipped it into his jacket pocket. He was starting out of the squad room when Carella called to him.

'Bert?'

Kling turned. 'Yeah?'

'You . . . you know how we feel about this, don't you?'

Kling nodded. 'I think I do.'

'OK.'

The two men stared at each other for a moment. Then Kling turned and walked rapidly out of the room.

The city is a crazy thing of many parts which don't quite fit together. You would think all the pieces would join, like the interlocking pieces of a jigsaw puzzle, but somehow the rivers and streams and bridges and tunnels separate and join areas which, in character and geography, could be foreign countries miles apart and not segments of the same sprawling metropolis.

Isola, of course, was the hub of the city, and the 87th Precinct was smack in the centre of that hub, like a wheel within a wheel, turning. Isola was an island, aptly and literally named by an unimaginative Italian explorer who had stumbled upon America, long after his compatriot had found it and claimed it for Queen Isabella. Columbus notwithstanding, the latterday adventurer had come upon this lovely island, had been struck speechless by its beauty, and had muttered simply, 'Isola'. Not 'Isola *Bella*' or 'Isola *Bellissima*' or 'Isola *la piu bella d'Italia*', but merely 'Isola'.

Island.

He had, since he had been a native Italian, born and raised in the tiny town of San Luigi, pronounced the name in perfect Italian. The name, if not the island itself, had been bastardized over the ensuing centuries, so that it was now pronounced 'Ice-a-luh', or sometimes even 'Ice-luh'. This mispronunciation might have disturbed the island's godfather had he been alive and kicking in the twentieth century, but chances are he wouldn't even have recognized the place. Isola was thronged with skyscrapers above ground, tunnels below the surface. She roared with the thunderous pace of big business. Her ports overflowed with goods from everywhere in the world. Her shores were laced with countless bridges connecting her to the rest of the less frenetic city. Isola had come a long way from San Luigi.

Majesta and Bethtown reflected the English influence on the new world, at least insofar as their names honoured British royalty. Bethtown had been named after the Virgin Queen in a burst of familiarity, the queen's ministers having decided to call the place 'Besstown'. But the man who delivered the new name to the crown colony was a man who'd lisped ever since he learned to talk, and he told the then-governor that it was the queen's desire to call this place 'Bethtown'. That's the way it went into the official records. By the time Bess discovered the monumental goof, the name had already gone into familiar usage, and she realized she couldn't very well re-educate the colonists, so she let it stand. Instead, she cut off the lisping messenger's head – but that's show biz.

Majesta had been named after George III, whose advisers at first thought it would be fitting to name the place Georgetown but who then decided there were too many Georgetowns around already. They dug into their Latin texts and came up with the word *majestas*, which meant, 'grandeur' or 'greatness' or 'majesty', and this seemed a proper tribute to their monarch. George later had a little trouble in Boston with some tea-drinkers, his majesty having diminished somewhat, but the name Majesta remained as a reminder of better days.

Calm's Point hadn't been named after anybody. In fact, for a very long time, hardly anyone at all lived on this small island bordering the larger island of Isola. In those days, wild animals foraged through the woods engaging each other in bloody battles – but the rest of the city nonetheless referred to the island across the River Harb as Calm's Point. A few hardy adventurers cleared the woods of beasts, pitched a couple of tents, and began propagating. That's the way to start a suburb, all right. After a while, when the tribe increases, you can petition the city for ferry service. In the event of a real population explosion, you can even hope for a bridge to the mainland.

Bert Kling was heading for Riverhead, where Mrs Joseph Wechsler made her residence. There was, in actuality, no river which had its head – or even its tail – in that part of the city. In the days of the old Dutch settlers the entire part of the city above Isola was owned by a patron named Ryerhert. Ryerhert's Farms was good land interspersed with igneous and metamorphic rock. As the city grew, Ryerhert sold part of his land

and donated the rest of it until eventually all of it was owned by the city. Ryerhert was hard to say. Even before 1917, when it became unfashionable for anything to sound even mildly Teutonic, Ryerhert had become Riverhead. There was, to be sure, water in Riverhead. But the water was a brook, really, and it wasn't even called a brook. It was called Five Mile Pond. It was not five miles wide, nor was it five miles long, nor was it five miles from any noticeable landmark. It was simply a brook which was called Five Mile Pond in a community called Riverhead which had no river's head in it.

The city was a crazy thing sometimes.

Mrs Wechsler lived in Riverhead in an apartment building which had a large entrance court flanked by two enormous stone flowerpots without any flowers in them. Kling walked between the pots, and through the entrance court, and into the vestibule. He found a name plate for Joseph Wechsler, apartment 4A, and pressed the bell. There was an answering click on the locked inner vestibule door. He opened the door and walked upstairs to the fourth floor.

He took a deep breath in the hallway outside the Wechsler apartment. Then he knocked.

A woman answered the knock.

She looked at Kling curiously and said, 'Yes?'

'Mrs Wechsler?'

'No?' It was still a question. 'Are you the new rabbi?' the woman asked.

'What?'

'The new . . .'

'No. I'm from the police.'

'Oh.' The woman paused. 'Oh, did you want to see Ruth?'

'Is that Mrs Wechsler?'

'Yes.'

'That's who I'd like to see,' Kling said.

'We . . .' The woman looked confused. 'She . . . you see, we're sitting *shivah*. That's . . . are you Jewish?'

'No.'

'We're in mourning. For Joseph. I'm his sister. I think it would be better if you came back another—'

'Ma'am, I'd appreciate it if I could talk to Mrs Wechsler now. I . . . I can understand . . . but . . .'

He suddenly wanted to leave. He did not want to intrude on mourners. And then he thought, Leave, and the killer gets an edge.

'Could I please see her now?' he asked. 'Would you please ask her?'

'I'll ask her,' the woman said, and she closed the door.

Kling waited in the hallway. He could hear the sounds of an apartment building everywhere around him, the sounds of life. And, beyond the closed door to apartment 4A, the stillness of death.

A young man came up the steps, carrying a book under his arm. He nodded solemnly at Kling, stopped just beside him, and asked, 'This is Wechsler?'

'Yes.'

'Thank you.'

He knocked on the door. While he waited for someone to answer his knock, he touched his fingers to the *mezuzah* fastened to the jamb. They waited together silently in the hallway. From somewhere upstairs a woman shouted to her son in the street. 'Martin! Come upstairs and put on a sweater!' Inside the apartment, there was silence. The young man knocked again. They could hear footsteps beyond the door. Joseph Wechsler's sister opened the door, looked first at Kling and then at the newcomer. 'Are you the rabbi?' she asked.

'Yes,' the man answered.

'Will you come in, please, *rov*?' she said. She turned to Kling. 'Ruth says she will talk to you, Mr – what is your name?'

'Kling.'

'Yes, Mr Kling. Mr Kling, she's just lost her husband. Would you please . . . could you kindly . . .?'

'I understand,' Kling said.

'Come in then. Please.'

They were sitting in the living room. There was a basket of fruit on the coffee table. The pictures, the mirrors were draped in black. The mourners sat on wooden crates. The men wore black *yomulkas*, the women wore shawls. The young rabbi had entered the room and was beginning to lead a prayer. Ruth Wechsler broke away from the mourners and came to Kling.

'How do you do?' she said. 'I am glad to know you.' She spoke with a thick Yiddish accent, which surprised Kling at first because she seemed like such a young woman and an unfamiliarity with English did not seem to go with youth. And then, looking at her more closely in the dimness of the room, he realized that she was well into her forties, perhaps even in her early fifties, one of those rare Semitic types who never truly age, with jet-black hair and luminous brown eyes, more luminous because they were wet with tears. She took his hand briefly, and he fumblingly shook hands, not knowing what to say, his own grief suddenly swallowed in the eyes of this beautiful pale woman who was ageless.

'Would you come with me, please?' she said. Her accent was really atrocious, almost a burlesque of the Sammy and Abie vaudeville routines, stripped of all amusement by the woman's utter sadness. Kling automatically made an aural adjustment, discounting the thick dialect, translating mentally, hearing still the curious structure of her sentences but cutting through the accent to arrive at the meaning of her words.

She led him to a small room behind the living room. There was a couch and a television set in the room. The screen was blank. Two windows faced the street and the sounds of a city in turbulence. From the living room came the sound of the rabbi's voice raised in the ancient Hebraic mourning prayers. In the small room with the television set Kling sat beside Ruth Wechsler and felt a oneness with the woman. He wanted to take her hands in his own. He wanted to weep with her.

'Mrs Wechsler, I know this is difficult—'

'No, I would like to talk to you,' she said. She pronounced the word 'vould'. She nodded and said, 'I want to help the police. We can't catch the killer unless I help the police.' He looked into the luminous brown eyes and heard the words exactly that way, even though she had actually said, 'Ve ken't ketch d'killuh onless I halp d'police.'

'Then . . . that's very kind of you, Mrs Wechsler. And I'll try not to ask too many questions. I'll try to be as brief as possible.'

'Take what time you need,' she said.

'Mrs Wechsler, would you happen to know what your husband was doing in Isola at that particular bookshop?'

'Nearby there, he has a store.'

'Where is that, Mrs Wechsler?'

'On the Stem and North Forty-seventh.'

'What kind of a store?'

'Hardware.'

'I see, and his store is close to the bookshop. Did he go to the bookshop often?'

'Yes. He was a big reader, Joseph. He doesn't speak too well, Joseph. He has, like me, a terrible accent. But he enjoyed reading. He said this helped him with words, to read it out loud. He would read to me out loud in bed. I think ... I think he went there to get a book I mentioned last week – that I said it would be nice if we read it.'

'What book was that, Mrs Wechsler?'

'By Herman Wouk, he's a fine man. Joseph read to me out loud *The Caine Mutiny* and *This Is My God*, and I said to him we should get this book, *Marjorie Morningstar*, because when it came out there was some fuss, some Jewish people took offence. I said to Joseph, how could such a fine man like Herman Wouk write a book would offend Jews? I said to Joseph there must be a mistake. There must be too many people, they're too sensitive. I said it must be that Mr Wouk is the offended party, that this man is being misunderstood, that his love is being misunderstood for something else. That's what I said to Joseph. So I asked him to get the book, we should find out for ourselves.'

'I see. And you think he went there to get that book?'

'Yes, I think so.'

'Was this a habit of his? Buying books in that particular store?'

'Buying there, and also using the rental library.'

'I see. But at *that* store? Not at a store in your own neighbourhood, for example?'

'No. Joseph spent a lot of time with his business, you see, and so he would do little errands on his lunch hour, or maybe before he came home, but always in the neighbourhood where he has his business.'

'What sort of errands do you mean, Mrs Wechsler?'

'Oh, like little things. Let me see. Well, like a few weeks ago, there was a portable radio we have, it needed fixing. So Joseph took it with him to work and had it fixed in a neighbourhood store there.'

'I see.'

'Or his automobile, it got a scratch in the fender. Just parked on the street, someone hit him and scraped paint from the fender – isn't there something we can do about that?'

'Well . . . have you contacted your insurance company?'

'Yes, but we have fifty-dollar deductible – you know what that is?'

'Yes.'

'And this was just a small paint job, twenty-five, thirty dollars, I forget. I still have to pay the bill. The car painter sent me his bill last week.'

'I see,' Kling said. 'In other words, your husband made a habit of dealing with businessmen in the neighbourhood where his own business was located. And someone could have known that he went to that bookshop often.'

'Yes. Someone could have known.'

'Is there anyone who . . . who might have had a reason for wanting to kill your husband, Mrs Wechsler?'

Quite suddenly, Ruth Wechsler said, 'You know, I can't get used to he's dead.' She said the words conversationally, as if she were commenting about a puzzling aspect of the weather. Kling fell silent and listened. 'I can't get used to he won't read to me any more out loud. In bed.' She shook her head. 'I can't get used to it.'

The room was silent. In the living room, the litany of the dead rose and fell in melodic, sombre tones.

'Did . . . did he have any enemies, Mrs Wechsler?' Kling asked softly.

Ruth Wechsler shook her head.

'Had he received any threatening notes or telephone calls?'

'No.'

'Had he had any arguments with anyone? Heated words? Anything like that?'

'I don't know. I don't think so.'

'Mrs Wechsler ... when your husband died ... at the hospital, the detective who was with him heard him say the word "carpenter". Is that the name of anyone you know?'

'No. Carpenter? No.' She shook her head. 'No, we don't know anybody by that name.'

'Well ... is it possible your husband was having some woodworking done?'

'No.'

'That he might have contacted a carpenter or a cabinetmaker?'

'No.'

'Nothing like that?'

Kling said, 'Are you sure?'

'I'm positive.'

'Do you have any idea why he would have said that word, Mrs Wechsler? He repeated it over and over. We thought it might have some special meaning.'

'No. Nobody.'

'Do you have any of your husband's letters or bills? Perhaps he was corresponding with someone, or doing business with someone who—'

'I shared everything with my husband. Nobody named Carpenter. No woodworkers. No cabinetmakers. I'm sorry.'

'Well, could I have the bills and letters anyway? I'll return them to you in good condition.'

'But please don't take too long with the bills,' Ruth Wechsler said. 'I like to pay bills prompt.' She sighed heavily. 'I have to read it now.'

'I'm sorry, what ...?'

'The book. Mr Wouk's book.' She paused. 'My poor husband,' she said. 'My poor darling.'

And though she pronounced the word 'dollink', it did not sound at all amusing.

In the hallway outside the apartment, Kling suddenly leaned back against the wall and squeezed his eyes shut. He breathed heavily and violently for several moments, and then he let out a long sigh, and shoved himself off the wall, and quietly went down the steps to the street.

It was Saturday, and the children were all home from school. A stickball game was in progress in the middle of the street, the boys wearing open shirts in the unaccustomed October balminess. Little girls in bright frocks skipped rope on the sidewalk – 'Double-ee-Dutch, Double-ee-Dutch, catch a rabbit and build a hutch!' Two little boys were playing marbles in the gutter, one of them arguing about the illegal use of a steelie in the game. Further up the street Kling saw three pint-sized conspirators, two boys and a girl, rush up to a doorway on street level, glance around furtively, ring the bell, and then rush across the street to the opposite side. As he passed the doorway, the door opened and a housewife peered out inquisitively. From across the street the three children began chanting, 'Lady, lady, *I* did it; lady, lady, *I* did it; lady, lady, *I* did it; lady, lady, *I* did it . . .'

The sound of their voices echoed in his ears all the way up the block.

7

Teddy Carella was talking.
She said:

'Yes?' Carella said.

66

'I'm beginning to get the message,' Carella said.

'Is that the best you can do?' Carella asked. 'That's not very original. So you love me, huh?'

Teddy repeated the three words, her hands rapidly spelling the message. He took her into his arms and kissed the tip of her nose briefly, and then his mouth dropped to hers and he kissed her completely and longingly, holding her in his arms after the kiss, her head cradled against his cheek. He released her at last and took off his jacket and then took his service revolver from his right rear pocket, unclipping the holster and putting the gun down on the end table. Teddy frowned and a torrent of words spilled from her hands.

'All right, all right,' Carella answered. 'I won't leave it around where the kids can get at it. Where are they, anyway?'

In the yard, her hands told him. *What happened today? Did you talk—*

But Carella had picked up the revolver and gone into the bedroom of the old Riverhead house, and he could no longer see her hands. She came into the room after him, turned him around to face her, and completed the sentence.

—to Kling? How is he?

Carella unbuttoned his shirt and threw it over one of the chairs. Teddy picked it up and carried it to the hamper. In the back yard he could hear the twins chasing each other, shouting their childish gibberish.

'I talked to Kling, yes,' he said. 'He's working on the case with us.'

Teddy frowned and then shrugged.

'I felt the same way, honey,' Carella answered. He took off his T-shirt, wiped perspiration from his chest and under his arms, and then fired the wadded shirt at the hamper, missing. Teddy cast him a baleful glance and picked up the shirt. 'But he wants in on it, and we can't very well refuse him.' He had turned his back, heading for the bathroom, thoughtlessly. He stopped in his tracks, turned to her, and repeated his words so that she could read his lips. 'We can't very well refuse him.'

Teddy nodded, but she still seemed troubled by the concept. She followed Carella into the bathroom and sat on the edge of the tub while he washed. Through a layer of suds and water, Carella said, 'We figure the killer was after one of the four he got, Teddy. Maybe we're wrong, but that's the way we read it.' His hands had covered his mouth on the last two words as he rinsed away suds. 'Read it,' he repeated, and Teddy nodded. He dried his face and then began speaking again while she watched his lips intently. 'We've been questioning relatives of the deceased. Meyer and I spoke to Mrs Land out on Sands Spit this morning, and Bert went to see Mrs Wechsler this afternoon. So far, there's nothing we can go on. There's Claire's father, of course, and Meyer and I thought we'd go see him tomorrow ...'

Teddy frowned instantly.

'What is it?' Carella asked.

The folks are coming tomorrow, she told him.

'What time?'

In the afternoon. One or two. For lunch.

'Then Meyer and I ... well, we'll make it early in the morning. He's got to be talked to, Teddy.'

Teddy nodded.

'We haven't been able to get a line on the third man who was killed in the shop. His name's Anthony La Scala, and his driver's licence gave an address in Isola for him. But Meyer and I checked there a little while ago, and the super told us he'd moved about a month ago. The post office doesn't have a forwarding address for him.'

That might be something, Teddy said.

'It might. I want to do some homework with the phone book later.'

Teddy shook her head.

'Why not?'

He moved a month ago. The phone book ...

'That's right,' Carella said, nodding. 'His new address and

number wouldn't be listed yet. How come you're so smart?' He grinned and held out his hands to her. She took them, and he pulled her from her sitting position and held her close to his naked chest. 'Why don't we have Fanny feed the kids and put them to bed?' he said. 'Then we can go out to dinner and a movie.'

Teddy wiggled her eyebrows.

'Well, yeah, that, too. But I thought later.'

She ran her tongue over her lips and then pulled away from him. He reached out for her, missed, and slapped her on the behind as she went out of the bathroom, laughing soundlessly. When he came into the bedroom, she was taking off her clothes.

'What are you doing?' he asked, puzzled. 'The kids are still awake.'

Teddy let her hands dangle loosely from the wrists and then waggled the fingers.

'Oh, you're gonna take a shower,' he said.

She nodded.

'I think you're just trying to tease me, that's all.'

Teddy shrugged speculatively and then went past him, half naked, into the bathroom. She closed the door, and he heard the lock clicking shut. The door opened again. She cocked her head around the door-frame, grinned mischievously, and then brought her right hand up suddenly. Quickly her fingers moved.

Go talk to your children, she said.

Then, at the end of the sentence, she waved good-bye, her head and hand disappeared, the door clicked shut, the lock snapped. In a moment, Carella heard the shower going. He smiled, put on a fresh T-shirt and went downstairs to find the twins and Fanny.

Fanny was sitting on a bench under the single huge tree in the Carella back yard, a big Irish woman in her early fifties who looked up the moment Carella came out of the house.

'Well,' she said, 'it's himself.'

'Daddy!' Mark yelled, his fist poised to sock his sister in the eye. He ran across the yard and leaped into Carella's arms. April, a little slower to respond, especially since she'd expected a punch just a moment before, did a small take and then shot across the lawn as if she'd been propelled from a launching pad. The twins were almost two and a half years old, fraternal twins who had managed to combine the best features of their parents in faces that looked similar but not identical. Both had Carella's high cheekbones and slanting oriental eyes. Both had Teddy's black hair and full mouths. At the moment, Mark also had a strangle hold on Carella's neck, and April was doing her best to climb to a sitting position on his waist by clambering up his legs.

'It's himself,' April said, mimicking Fanny, from whom she heard most of her English during the day.

'It's himself indeed,' Carella said. 'How come you weren't waiting at the front door to greet me?'

'Well, who knows when you minions of the law will come home?' Fanny asked smiling.

'Sure, who knows when the minnows,' April said.

'Well, Daddy,' Mark said seriously, 'How was business today?'

'Fine, just fine,' Carella said.

'Did you catch a crook?' April asked.

'No, not yet.'

'Will you catch . . .' She paused and rephrased it. 'Will you catch . . .' Apparently the rephrasing didn't satisfy her either. 'Will you catch . . .' she said, paused again, gave it up, and then completed the sentence. 'Will you catch one tomorrow?'

'Oh, if the weather's good, maybe we will,' Carella said.

'Well, that's good, Daddy,' Mark said.

' "*If* the weather's good," he said,' April put in.

'Well, if you catch one, bring him home,' Mark said.

'Those two are gonna be G men,' Fanny said. She sat in bright, redheaded splendour under the bold autumn foliage of the tree, grinning approval at her brood. A trained nurse who supplemented the meagre salary Carella could afford by taking night calls whenever she could, she had been working for the Carellas ever since the twins were brought home from the hospital.

'Daddy, what do crooks look like?' Mark asked.

'Well, some of them look like Fanny,' Carella said.

'That's right, teach them,' Fanny said.

'Are there lady crooks?' April asked.

'There are lady crooks and men crooks, yes,' Carella said.

'But no chi'drun,' Mark said. He always had difficulty with the word.

'Children,' Fanny corrected, as she invariably did.

'Chi'drun,' Mark repeated, and he nodded.

'No, no children crooks,' Carella said. 'Children are too smart to be crooks.' He put the twins down and said, 'Fanny, I brought you something.'

'What?'

'A swear box.'

'What in hell is a swear box?'

'I left it in the kitchen for you. You've got to put money in it every time you use a swear word.'

'Like hell I will.'

'Like hell she will,' April said.

'See?' Carella said.

'I don't know where they pick it up,' Fanny answered, shaking her head in mock puzzlement.

'You feel like giving us the night off?' Carella asked.

'It's Saturday, ain't it? Young people have to go out on Saturday.'

'Good,' Mark said.

'Huh?' Carella asked.

'We're young people.'

'Yes, but Fanny's going to feed you and put you to bed, and Mommy and Daddy are going to a movie.'

'Which one?'

'I don't know yet.'

'Go see a monster fimm,' Mark said.

'A what?'

'A monster fimm.'

'Film?'

'Yeah.'

'Why should I? I have two monsters right here.'

'Don't, Daddy,' April said. 'You'll scare us.'

He sat with them in the yard while Teddy showered and dusk claimed the city. He read to them from *Winnie the Pooh* until it was time for their dinner. Then he went upstairs to change his clothes. He and Teddy had a good dinner and saw a good movie. When they got home to the old Riverhead house, they made love. He leaned back against the pillow afterwards and smoked a cigarette in the dark.

And somehow Kling's loss seemed enormously magnified.

728 Peterson Avenue was in the heart of Riverhead in a good middle-class neighbourhood dotted with low apartment buildings and two-storey frame houses. Ralph Townsend lived there in apartment number 47. At nine o'clock on Sunday morning, October 15, Detectives Meyer Meyer and Steve Carella rang the bell outside the closed door and waited. Kling had told them the night before that Claire's father was a night watchman, and he'd advised them to call at the apartment around nine o'clock, when the old man would be returning home from his shift and before he went to bed. As it was, they caught Townsend in the middle of breakfast. He invited them into the apartment and then poured coffee for them. They sat together in the small kitchen, with sunlight streaming through the window and burnishing the oilcloth on the table. Townsend was in his middle fifties, a man with all his hair, as black as his daughter's had been. He had a huge barrel chest and muscular arms. He wore a white shirt, the sleeves rolled up over his biceps. He wore bright-green suspenders. He also wore a black tie.

'I won't be going to sleep today,' he said. 'I have to go over to the funeral parlour.'

'You went to work last night, Mr Townsend?' Meyer asked.

'A man has to work,' Townsend said simply. 'I mean ... well, you didn't know Claire, but . . . well, you see, in this family, we thought . . . her mother died when she was just a little girl, you know, and . . . we . . . we sort of made up between us that what we owed to Mary . . . that was her name, Claire's mother . . . we made up that what we owed to Mary was to *live*, you see. To carry on. To *live*. So . . . I feel I owe the same thing to Claire. I owe it to her to . . . to miss her with all my heart, but to go on living. And working is a part of life.' He fell silent. Then he said, 'So I went to work last night.' And he fell silent again. He sipped at his coffee. 'Last night I went to work, and today I'll go to the funeral parlour where my little girl is lying dead.' He sipped at the coffee again. He was a strong man, and the grief on his face was strong, in keeping with his character. There were no tears in his eyes, but sorrow sat within him like a heavy stone.

'Mr Townsend,' Carella said, 'we have to ask you some questions. I know you'll understand . . .'

'I understand,' Townsend said, 'but I'd like to ask you a question first, if that's all right.'

'Sure,' Carella said.

'I want to know . . . did this have anything to do with Bert?'

'What do you mean?'

'I like Bert,' Townsend said. 'I liked him the minute Claire brought him around. He did wonders for her, you know. She'd been through that thing where her boyfriend was killed, and for a while she . . . she forgot about living, do you know what I mean? I thought . . . I thought we'd agreed on . . . on what to do when her mother died, and then . . . then this fellow she was going with got killed in the war, and Claire just slipped away. Just slipped away. Until Bert came along – and then she changed. She became herself again. She was alive again. Now . . .'

'Yes, Mr Townsend?'

'Now, I . . . I wonder. I mean, Bert's a cop and I like Bert. I like him. But . . . did . . . did Claire get killed because her boyfriend is a cop? That's what I'd like to know.'

'We don't think so, Mr Townsend.'

'Then why did she get killed? I've been over it a hundred

times in my mind. And it seems to me that . . . maybe somebody had something against Bert and he took it out on Claire. He killed Claire to get even with Bert. Just because Bert's a cop. Now doesn't that seem to make sense? If anything in this whole damn thing makes sense, doesn't that seem to make the most sense?'

'We haven't overlooked that possibility, Mr Townsend,' Meyer said. 'We've gone back in our files over all the major arrests Bert made. We've eliminated those which were petty offences because they didn't seem to warrant such massive retaliation. We've also eliminated any men or women who are still in prison, since obviously—'

'Yes, I understand.'

'—and also those who were paroled more than a year ago. We figure a vendetta murder would have been committed as soon after—'

'Yes, I see, I see,' Townsend said.

'So we've rounded up recent parolees and men who've completed shorter terms – at least, all those for whom we have known residences. We're still in the process of questioning these people. But, quite frankly, this doesn't seem to be *that* kind of a murder.'

'How do you know?'

'A murder case has a feel to it, Mr Townsend. When you've worked enough of them, you develop a sort of intuition. We don't think Claire's death was connected with the fact that Bert is a cop. We may be wrong, but so far our thinking is going in another direction.'

'What direction is that?' Townsend asked.

'Well, we think the killer was after a specific person in that shop, and that he got the one he was after.'

'Why couldn't it have been Claire? And why couldn't . . .?'

'It *could* have been Claire, Mr Townsend.'

'Then it also could have been connected to Bert.'

'Yes, but then why didn't the killer go after Bert? Why would he kill Claire?'

'I don't know why. What kind of a crazy twisted bastard would kill four people anyway?' Townsend asked. 'Are you

74

trying to apply logic to this? What logic is there? You just told me he was after only *one* person, for Christ's sake, but he killed *four*!'

Meyer sighed patiently. 'Mr Townsend, we haven't discounted the possibility that someone carrying a grudge against Bert Kling took it out on him by killing your daughter. It's happened before, certainly, and we're investigating that possibility. I'm only trying to say that it doesn't seem to be the most fruitful course we can pursue in this case. That's all. But, of course, we'll continue to explore the possibility until we've exhausted it.'

'I'd like to think Bert had nothing to do with this,' Townsend said.

'Then please think that,' Carella said.

'I'd like to.'

The room was silent.

'In any case,' Meyer said, 'Claire was one of the four people killed. With this in mind—'

'You're wondering whether Claire was the intended victim?'

'Yes, sir. That's what we're wondering.'

'How would I know?'

'Well, Mr Townsend,' Carella said, 'we thought perhaps Claire might have mentioned something that was troubling her. Or—'

'Nothing seemed to be troubling her.'

'Had she received any threatening phone calls? Or letters? Would you know?'

'I work nights,' Townsend said. 'I'm usually asleep during the day while Claire is at school or doing casework. We usually have dinner together, but I don't recall her saying anything about threats. Nothing like that.' He had inadvertently slipped into the present tense in discussing his daughter, casually sidestepping the fact that she was dead.

'What sort of casework did she do?' Carella asked, reverting to the proper tense.

'She works at Buenavista Hospital,' Townsend said.

'What sort of work?'

'Well, you know she's a social worker, don't you?'

'Yes, but—'

'She does ... well, you *know* what medical social workers do, don't you?'

'Not exactly, Mr Townsend.'

'Well, Claire works—' He stopped suddenly, as if realizing all at once that he had been committing an error in tense. He stared at the detectives, somewhat surprised by his own discovery. He sighed heavily. 'Claire *worked*,' he said, and he hesitated again, giving the word time to set, accepting the knowledge once and for all, 'Claire worked with hospitalized patients. Doctors provide medical care, you know, but very often it takes more than that to make a patient well. Claire provided the something more. She helped the patient towards *using* the medical care, towards *wanting* to be well again.'

'I see,' Carella said. He thought for a moment and then asked, 'Did Claire ever mention any particular patient she was working with?'

'Yes, she mentioned a great many of them.'

'In what way, Mr Townsend?'

'Well, she took a personal interest in *all* the people she worked with. In fact, you might say her work *was* this personal interest, this special attention to a patient's problems.'

'And she would come home and tell you about these people, is that right?'

'Yes. Stories about them ... or ... or funny things that happened. You know.'

'Were there times when something happened that wasn't so funny, Mr Townsend?'

'Oh, she had her complaints. She was carrying a very large caseload, and sometimes it got a little difficult. Sometimes her temper wore a little thin.'

'Did she mention any specific trouble?'

'Trouble?'

'With patients? With families of patients? With doctors? With anyone on the hospital staff?'

'No, nothing specific.'

'Anything at all? A slight argument? Anything you can remember?'

'I'm sorry. Claire got along well with people, you see. I guess that's why she was a good social worker. She got along with people. She treated *everyone* like a person. That's a rare talent, Mr Carella.'

'It is,' Carella agreed. 'Mr Townsend, you've been very helpful. Thank you very much.'

'Is . . . is there anything I can tell Bert?' Townsend asked.

'I beg your pardon?'

'Bert. He's sure to be at the funeral parlour.'

On the way downstairs, Meyer asked, 'What do you think?'

'I'd like to hit the hospital,' Carella said. 'What time do you have?'

'Ten-thirty.'

'You game?'

'Sarah said to be home by lunch.' Meyer shrugged.

'Let's do it now, then. It might give us something to go on tomorrow.'

'I don't like hospitals,' Meyer said. 'My mother died in a hospital.'

'If you want me to go alone . . .'

'No, no, I'll come with you. It's just I don't like hospitals, that's all.'

They walked to the police sedan, and Carella slipped in behind the wheel. He started the car and then eased it into the light Sunday morning traffic.

'Let's have a quick run-down while we drive over, OK?' he said.

'OK.'

'What's the other team covering?'

'Di Maeo's checking out the 1954 bookstore holdup. Our records show the thief was released from Castleview in 1956 and returned to Denver. But he wants to make sure the guy didn't come back here. He's checking on some of his buddies, too, to make sure they weren't involved in the Friday shooting.'

'What else?'

'He's going over every arrest Bert ever made, sorting them

out, putting a pickup-and-hold on anybody who looks like a possible. He's plenty busy, Steve.'

'OK. What about Willis and Brown?'

'Willis is trying to locate family or friends of the fourth victim. What the hell was his name?'

'La Scala.'

'That's right,' Meyer said. 'Anthony La Scala.'

'How come Italians are always getting shot?' Carella asked.

'They're not.'

'On *The Untouchables* they're always getting shot.'

'Well, that show is stacked,' Meyer said. He grinned slyly and added, 'Did you catch that one?'

'I caught it.'

'Stacked. Robert Sta—'

'I caught it,' Carella said again. 'Has Willis found an address for this La Scala character yet?'

'Not yet.'

'That's pretty peculiar, isn't it?'

'Yeah, pretty peculiar.'

'Makes him sound a little shady.'

'All your countrymen are shady,' Meyer said. 'Didn't you know that? Don't you watch *The Untouchables*?'

'Sure I do. You know what I noticed?'

'What?'

'Robert Stack never smiles.'

'I saw him smile once,' Meyer said.

'When?'

'I forget. He was killing some hood. But I distinctly saw him smile.'

'I never saw him smile,' Carella said seriously.

'Well, a cop's life is a tough one,' Meyer said. 'You know what I noticed?'

'What?'

'Frank Nitti always wears the same striped, double-breasted suit.'

'That's 'cause crime doesn't pay,' Carella said.

'I like that guy who plays Nitti.'

'Yeah, I do, too.' Carella nodded. 'You know something? I don't think I ever saw *him* smile either.'

'What's with you and this smiling business?'

'I don't know. I like to see people smile every now and then.'

'Here,' Meyer said. 'Here's a smile for you.' He grinned from ear to ear.

Carella said, 'Here's the hospital. Save your teeth for the admissions nurse.'

The admissions nurse was charmed to pieces by Meyer's dazzling dental display, and she told them how to reach the ward where Claire Townsend had worked. The intern on duty wasn't quite as thrilled by Meyer's smile. He was underpaid and overworked, and he didn't need a comic vaudeville team lousing up his nice quiet ward on a nice quiet Sunday morning. He was ready to give the itinerant flatfoots a fast brush, but he didn't know he was dealing with Detective Meyer Meyer, scourge of the underworld and the medical profession, the most patient cop and man in the city, if not in the entire United States.

'We're terribly sorry to intrude on your valuable time, Dr McElroy,' Meyer said, 'but—'

McElroy, who was a bit of a sharpshooter himself, quickly said, 'Well, I'm glad you understand, gentlemen. If you'll kindly leave, then, we can all get back to—'

'Yes, we understand,' Meyer sniped, 'and of course you have patients to examine and sedatives to distribute and—'

'You're oversimplifying an intern's work,' McElroy said.

'Naturally I am, and I apologize, because I know how very busy you are, Dr McElroy. But we're dealing with a homicide here—'

'I'm dealing with sick people here,' McElroy interrupted.

'And your job is to keep them from dying. But our job is to find out who killed the ones who are already dead. Anything you can tell us about—'

'I have specific orders from the Chief of Staff,' McElroy said, 'and it's my job to carry them out in his absence. A hospital works by the clock, Detective . . . Meyer, was it?'

'Yes, and I understand—'

'—and I simply haven't the time to answer a lot of questions –

not this morning, I haven't. Why don't you wait until Staff comes in, and you can ask—'

'But you worked with Claire Townsend, didn't you?'

'Claire worked with me, and with all the other doctors on this ward, and also with Staff. Look, Detective Meyer—'

'Did you get along well with her?'

'I don't intend to answer any questions, Detective Meyer.'

'I guess he didn't get along with her, Steve,' Meyer said.

'Of *course* I got along with her. Everyone did. Claire was a ... look, Detective Meyer, you're not going to trick me into a long discussion about Claire. Really! I have work to do. I have patients.'

'I have patience, too,' Meyer said, and he grinned beautifully, 'You were saying about Claire?'

McElroy glared at Meyer silently.

'I guess we could subpoena him,' Carella said.

'Subpoena me? What in hell ...? Look,' McElroy said patiently, 'I have to make my rounds at eleven o'clock. Then I have to order medication. Then I have two—'

'Yes, we know you're busy,' Meyer said.

'I have two spinal taps and some intravenouses, not to mention new admissions and personal histories and—'

'Let's go get a warrant,' Carella said.

McElroy's shoulders slumped. 'Why'd I ever become a doctor?' he asked no one in particular.

'How long did you know Claire?'

'About six months,' McElroy said tiredly.

'Did you like working with her?'

'Everyone did. Medical social workers are very valuable to us, and Claire was an unusually conscientious and able person. I was sorry to read about ... about what happened. Claire was a nice girl. And a good worker.'

'Did she ever have any trouble with anyone on the ward?'

'No.'

'Doctors? Nurses? Patients?'

'No.'

'Now, come on, Dr McElroy,' Meyer said. 'This girl wasn't a saint.'

'Maybe she wasn't a saint,' McElroy said, 'but she was a damn good social worker. And a good social worker doesn't get involved in petty squabbles.'

'*Are* there petty squabbles on this ward?'

'There are petty squabbles everywhere.'

'But Claire never got involved in any of them.'

'Not to my knowledge,' McElroy said.

'How about her patients? You can't tell us all of her patients were ideal, well-adjusted individuals who—'

'No, many of them were quite disturbed.'

'Then, surely, *all* of them didn't readily accept what she was trying to—'

'That's true. Not all of them accepted her at first.'

'Then there *were* problems.'

'At first. But Claire had a wonderful way with people, and she almost always gained a patient's complete confidence.'

'*Almost* always?'

'Yes.'

'When didn't she?' Carella asked.

'What?'

'Almost isn't always, Dr McElroy. *Did* she have trouble with any of the patients?'

'Nothing serious. Nothing she couldn't work out. I'm trying to tell you that Claire was an unusually dedicated person who had a wonderful way of dealing with her patients. To be quite frank about it, some medical social workers are a severe pain in the ass. But not Claire. Claire was gentle and patient and kind and understanding and ... she was *good*, period. She knew her job, and she loved her job. She was good at it. That's all I can tell you. Why, she even ... her work extended beyond this ward. She took a personal interest in the patients' families. She visited homes, helped relatives to make adjustments. She was an unusual person, believe me.'

'Which homes did she visit?'

'What?'

'Which homes did she—'

'Oh, I'm not sure. Several. I can't remember.'

'Try.'

'Really ...'

'Try.'

'Oh, let me see. There was a man in, several months back, had broken his leg on the job. Claire took an interest in his family, visited the home, helped the children. Or the beginning of last month, for example. We had a woman in with a ruptured appendix. Quite a mess, believe me. Peritonitis, subdiaphragmatic abscess, the works. She was here quite a while – just released last week, as a matter of fact. Claire got very friendly with her young daughter, a girl of about sixteen. Even kept up her interest after the woman was discharged.'

'What do you mean?'

'She called her.'

'The young girl? She called her from here? From the ward?'

'Yes.'

'What did she talk about?'

'I'm sure I don't know. I'm not in the habit of listening to other people's—'

'How often did she call her?'

'Well ... quite frequently this past week.' McElroy paused. 'In fact, the girl called *her* once. Right here.'

'She did, huh? What's the girl's name?'

'I don't know. I can get you the mother's name. That would be in our records.'

'Yes, would you please?' Carella said.

'This is a little unusual, isn't it?' Meyer asked. 'Keeping up contact with a woman's daughter after the woman's been released?'

'No, not terribly unusual. Most social workers do a follow-up. And as I said, Claire was a very conscientious—'

'But would you say there was a *personal* involvement with this young girl?'

'All of Claire's involvements—'

'Please, Dr McElroy, I think you know what I mean. Was Claire Townsend's interest in this young girl more than the interest she usually expressed in a patient or the family of a patient?'

82

McElroy thought this one over for a few minutes. Then he said, 'Yes, I would say so.'

'Good. May we look at those records now, please?'

Back at the squad, Detective Hal Willis was studying a necropsy report made on the dead body of Anthony La Scala. The report informed him that the cause of death had been three .45-calibre bullets in the lungs and heart and that death had most probably been instantaneous. But the report also mentioned the fact that both of La Scala's arms were scarred around the superficial veins on the flexor surface of the forearm and the bend of the elbow. These scars appeared to be short ropelike thickenings of the dermis from three-eighths of an inch to one inch in length and about three-sixteenths of an inch wide. It was the opinion of the medical examiner, strongly bolstered by a large amount of heroin found in La Scala's blood stream, that the marks on his arms were mainline scars, that La Scala had injected the drug intravenously, and that he had undoubtedly been addicted to the drug for a good long time, judging from the number of scars and the tiny dots arranged seriatim on the thickened areas.

Willis put the report into the Kling Case folder and then said to Brown, who was sitting at the next desk, 'That's great, ain't it? A goddamn hophead. How do we find out where a hophead was living? Probably in Grover Park underneath a goddamn bench! How do we find the friends and relatives of a goddamn hophead?'

Brown considered this pensively for a moment. Then he said, 'Maybe it's a break, Hal. *This* may have been the one he wanted. Hopheads get mixed up in a lot of crazy things.' He nodded again, emphatically. 'Maybe this is a break.'

And maybe it was.

9

Monday morning came.

It always does.

On Monday morning you sit back and take a look at things, and things look lousy. That's a part of Monday, the nature of the beast. Monday should be a fresh beginning, a sort of road-company New Year's Day. But, somehow, Monday is only and always a continuation, a familiar awakening to a start which is really only a repetition. There should be laws against Monday morning.

Arthur Brown didn't like Monday morning any more than anyone else did. He was a cop, and only incidentally a Negro, and he lived in a coloured ghetto close to the office. He had a wife named Caroline, and a daughter named Connie, and they shared a four-room flat in a building weary with time. Happily, when Brown got out of bed on the morning of October 16, the floors were not cold. The floors were usually cold around this time of year, despite the city ordinance which made it mandatory to provide steam heat beginning on the fifteenth of October. This year, with Indian summer swinging her hot little behind through the city, the landlords were enjoying a reprieve, and the tenants didn't have to bang on the radiators. Brown was grateful for the warm floors.

He got out of bed quietly, not wanting to wake Caroline, who was asleep beside him. He was a big man with close-cropped black hair and brown eyes and a deep-brown complexion. He had worked on the docks before he joined the force, and his arms and shoulders and chest still bulged with the muscles of his youthful labour. He had been sleeping in his pyjama bottoms, Caroline curled beside him in the over-large top. After he silently slipped out of bed, he walked bare-chested into the kitchen, where he filled a kettle with water and put it on the stove. He turned on the radio very softly and listened to the news broadcast as he shaved. Race riots in the Congo. Sit-in demonstrations in the South. Apartheid in South Africa.

He wondered why he was black.

He often wondered this. He wondered it idly, and with no real conviction that he *was* black. That was the strange part of it. When Arthur Brown looked in the mirror, he saw only himself. Now he knew he was a Negro, yes. But he was also a Democrat, and a detective, and a husband, and a father, and he read *The New York Times* – he was a lot of things. And so he wondered why he was black. He wondered why, being this variety of things besides being black, people would look at him and see Arthur Brown, Negro – and not Arthur Brown, detective, or Arthur Brown, husband, or any of the Arthur Browns who had nothing to do with the fact that he was black. This was not a simple concept, and Brown did not equate it in simple Shakespearian-Shylock terms, which the world had long outgrown.

When Brown looked into his mirror he saw a person.

It was the world who had decided that this person was a black man. Being this person was an extremely difficult thing, because it meant living a life the world had decided upon, and not the life he – Arthur Brown – would particularly have chosen. He, Arthur Brown, did not see a black man or a white man or a yellow man or a chartreuse man when he looked into his mirror.

He saw Arthur Brown.

He saw himself.

But superimposed upon this image of himself was the external concept of black man–white man, a concept which existed and which Brown was forced to accept. He became a person playing a complicated role. He looked at himself and saw Arthur Brown, Man. That's all he wanted to be. He had no desire to be white. In fact, he rather liked the warm, burnished colour of his own skin. He had no desire to go to bed with a creamy-skinned blonde. He had heard coloured friends of his state that white men had bigger sex organs than Negroes, but he didn't believe it, and he felt no envy. He had encountered prejudice in a hundred and one subtle and unsubtle ways from the moment he was old enough to understand what was being said and done around him, but the intolerance never left him feeling angry – it only confused him.

You see, he thought, I'm me, Arthur Brown. Now what is all this white man–black man crap? I don't understand what you want me to be. *You* are saying I'm a Negro, *you* are telling me this is so, but *I* don't know what Negro means, I don't know what this whole damn discussion is all about. What do you want from me, exactly? If I say, why yes, that's right, I'm a Negro, well, *then* what? What the hell is it you want, that's what I'd like to know.

Arthur Brown finished shaving, rinsed his face, and looked into the mirror.

As usual, he saw himself.

He dressed quietly, drank some orange juice and coffee, kissed his daughter as she lay sleeping in her crib, woke Caroline briefly to tell her he was off to work, and then went cross town to the neighbourhood where Joseph Wechsler had run a hardware store.

It was purely by chance that Meyer Meyer went to see Mrs Rudy Glennon alone that Monday morning, the chance having been occasioned by the fact that Steve Carella had drawn Lineup duty. Things might have worked out differently had Carella been along, but the police commissioner felt it was necessary to acquaint his working dicks with criminals every Monday to Thursday inclusive. Carella, being a working dick, took the Lineup duty like a man and sent Meyer to Mrs Glennon's apartment alone.

Mrs Glennon was the name supplied by Dr McElroy at Buenavista Hospital, the woman with whose family Claire Townsend had been personally involved. She lived in one of the worst slum sections in Isola, some five blocks from the station house. Meyer walked over, found the apartment building, and climbed the steps to the third floor. He knocked on the door to the apartment and waited.

'Who is it?' a voice called.

'Police,' Meyer called.

'What do you want? I'm in bed.'

'I'd like to talk to you, Mrs Glennon,' Meyer said.

'Come back next week. I'm sick. I'm in bed.'

'I'd like to talk to you now, Mrs Glennon.'

'What about?'

'Mrs Glennon, would you open the door, please?'

'Oh, for the love of Mary, it's open,' she shouted. 'Come in, come in.'

Meyer turned the knob and stepped into the apartment. The shades were drawn and the room he entered was dim. He peered into the apartment.

'I'm in here,' Mrs Glennon said. 'The bedroom.'

He followed the voice into the other room. She was sitting in the middle of a large double bed, propped against the pillows, a small faded woman wearing a faded pink robe over her nightgown. She looked at Meyer as if even the glance sapped all her energy. Her hair was stringy, threaded with grey strands. Her cheeks were gaunt.

'I told you I was sick,' Mrs Glennon said. 'What is it you want?'

'I'm sorry to bother you, Mrs Glennon,' Meyer said. 'The hospital told us you'd been released. I thought—'

'I'm convalescing,' she interrupted. She said the word proudly, as if she had learned it at great expense.

'Well, I'm awfully sorry. But if you feel you can answer a few questions, I'd appreciate it,' Meyer said.

'You're here now. I might as well.'

'You have a daughter, Mrs Glennon?'

'*And* a son. Why?'

'How old are the children?'

'Eileen is sixteen and Terry is eighteen. Why?'

'Where are they now, Mrs Glennon?'

'What's it to you? They haven't done anything wrong.'

'I didn't say they had, Mrs Glennon. I simply—'

'Then why do you want to know where they are?'

'Actually, we're trying to locate—'

'I'm here, Mom,' a voice behind Meyer said. The voice came suddenly, startling him. His hand automatically went for the service revolver clipped to his belt on the left – and then stopped. He turned slowly. The boy standing behind him was undoubtedly Terry Glennon, a strapping youth of eighteen, with his mother's piercing eyes and narrow jaw.

'What do you want, mister?' he said.

'I'm a cop,' Meyer told him before he got any wild ideas. 'I want to ask your mother a few questions.'

'My mother just got out of the hospital. She can't answer no questions,' Terry said.

'It's all right, son,' Mrs Glennon said.

'You let me handle this, Mom. You better go, mister.'

'Well, I'd like to ask—'

'I think you better go,' Terry said.

'I'm sorry, sonny,' Meyer said, 'but I happen to be investigating a homicide, and *I* think I'll stay.'

'A homi ...' Terry Glennon swallowed the information silently. 'Who got killed?'

'Why? Who do you *think* got killed?'

'I don't know.'

'Then why'd you ask?'

'I don't know. You said a homicide, so I naturally asked—'

'Uh-huh,' Meyer said. 'You know anyone named Claire Townsend?'

'No.'

'I know her,' Mrs Glennon said. 'Did she send you here?'

'Look, mister,' Terry interrupted, apparently making up his mind once and for all, 'I told you my mother's sick. I don't care *what* you're investigating – she ain't gonna—'

'Terry, now stop it,' his mother said. 'Did you buy the milk I asked you to?'

'Yeah.'

'Where is it?'

'I put it on the table.'

'Well, what good is it gonna do me on the table, where I can't get at it? Put some in a pot and turn up the gas. Then you can go.'

'What do you mean, go?'

'Downstairs. With your friends.'

'What do you mean, my *friends*? Why do you always say it that way?'

'Terry, do what I tell you.'

'You gonna let this guy tire you out?'

'I'm not tired.'

'You're sick!' Terry shouted. 'You just had an operation, for Christ's sake!'

'Terry, don't swear in my house,' Mrs Glennon said, apparently forgetting that she had profaned Christ's mother earlier, when Meyer was standing in the hallway. 'Now go put the milk on to heat and go downstairs and find something to do.'

'Boy, I don't understand you,' Terry said. He shot a petulant glare at his mother, some of it spilling on to Meyer, and then walked angrily out of the room. He picked up the container of milk from the table, went into the kitchen, banged around a lot of pots, and then stormed out of the apartment.

'He's got a temper,' Mrs Glennon said.

'Mmmmm,' Meyer commented.

'*Did* Claire send you here?'

'No, ma'am. Claire Townsend is dead.'

'What? What are you saying?'

'Yes, Ma'am.'

'Tch,' Mrs Glennon said. She tilted her head to one side and then repeated the sound again. 'Tch.'

'Were you very friendly with her, Mrs Glennon?' Meyer asked.

'Yes.' Her eyes seemed to have gone blank. She was thinking of something, but Meyer didn't know what. He had seen this look a great many times before, a statement triggering off a memory or an association, the person being interrogated simply drifting off into a private thought. 'Yes, Claire was a nice girl,' Mrs Glennon said, but her mind was on something else, and Meyer would have given his eyeteeth to have known what.

'She worked with you at the hospital, isn't that right?'

'Yes,' Mrs Glennon said.

'And with your daughter, too.'

'What?'

'Your daughter. I understand Claire was friendly with her.'

'Who told you that?'

'The intern at Buenavista.'

'Oh,' Mrs Glennon nodded. 'Yes, they were friendly,' she admitted.

'Very friendly?'

'Yes. Yes, I suppose so.'

'What is it, Mrs Glennon?'

'Huh? What?'

'What are you thinking about?'

'Nothing. I'm answering your questions. When ... when did ... when was Claire killed?'

'Friday evening,' Meyer said.

'Oh, then she—' Mrs Glennon closed her mouth.

'Then she what?' Meyer asked.

'Then she ... she was killed Friday evening,' Mrs Glennon said.

'Yes.' Meyer watched her face carefully. 'When was the last time you saw her, Mrs Glennon?'

'At the hospital.'

'And your daughter?'

'Eileen? I ... I don't know when she saw Claire last.'

'Where is she now, Mrs Glennon? At school?'

'No. No, she ... she's spending a few ... uh ... days with my sister. In Bethtown.'

'Doesn't she go to school, Mrs Glennon?'

'Yes, certainly she does. But I had the appendicitis, you know, and ... uh ... she stayed with my sister while I was in the hospital ... and ... uh ... I thought I ought to send her there for a while now, until I can get on my feet. You see?'

'I see. What's your sister's name, Mrs Glennon?'

'Iris.'

'Yes. Iris what?'

'Iris ... why do you want to know?'

'Oh, just for the record,' Meyer said.

'I don't want you to bother her, mister. She's got troubles enough of her own. She doesn't even know Claire. I wish you wouldn't bother her.'

'I don't intend to, Mrs Glennon.'

Mrs Glennon frowned. 'Her name is Iris Mulhare.'

Meyer jotted the name into his pad. 'And the address?'

'Look, you said—'

'For the record, Mrs Glennon.'

'1131 Fifty-sixth Street.'

'In Bethtown?'

'Yes.'

'Thank you. And you say your daughter Eileen is with her, is that right?'

'Yes.'

'When did she go there, Mrs Glennon?'

'Saturday. Saturday morning.'

'And she was there earlier, too, is that right? While you were in the hospital.'

'Yes.'

'Where did she meet Claire, Mrs Glennon?'

'At the hospital. She came to visit me one day while Claire was there. That's where they met.'

'Uh-huh,' Meyer said. 'And did Claire visit her at your sister's home? In Bethtown?'

'What?'

'I said I suppose Claire visited her at your sister's home.'

'Yes, I . . . I suppose so.'

'Uh-huh,' Meyer said. 'Well, that's very interesting, Mrs Glennon, and I thank you. Tell me, haven't you seen a newspaper?'

'No, I haven't.'

'Then you didn't know Claire was dead until I told you, is that right?'

'That's right.'

'Do you suppose Eileen knows?'

'I . . . I don't know.'

'Well, did she mention anything about it Saturday morning? Before she left for your sister's?'

'No.'

'Were you listening to the radio?'

'No.'

'Because it was on the air, you know. Saturday morning.'

'We weren't listening to the radio.'

'I see. And your daughter didn't see a newspaper before she left the house?'

'No.'

'But, of course, she must know about it by now. Has she said anything about it to you?'

'No.'

'You've spoken to her, haven't you? I mean, she does call you. From your sister's?'

'Yes, I . . . I speak to her.'

'When did you speak to her last, Mrs Glennon?'

'I . . . I'm very tired now. I'd like to rest.'

'Certainly. When did you speak to her last?'

'Yesterday,' Mrs Glennon said, and she sighed deeply.

'I see. Thank you, Mrs Glennon, you've been very helpful. Shall I get you that milk? It's probably warm enough by now.'

'Would you?'

Meyer went into the kitchen. The stove was set alongside a cabinet and a wall. A small cork bulletin board was nailed to the wall. A telephone rested on the cabinet. He took the pot of milk from the stove just as it was ready to overboil. He poured a cupful and then called, 'Do you want a lump of butter in this?'

'Yes, please.'

He opened the refrigerator, took out the butter dish, found a knife in the cabinet drawer, and was slicing off a square when he saw the hand-lettered note pinned to the bulletin board. The note read:

CLAIRE
SATURDAY
271 SOUTH FIRST STREET

He nodded once, briefly, silently copied the address into his pad, and then carried the buttered milk to Mrs Glennon. She thanked him for his kindness, asked him again not to bother her sister, and then began sipping at the cup.

Meyer left the apartment, wondering why Mrs Glennon had lied to him. He was still wondering about it when he reached the first-floor landing.

The attack came swiftly and silently.

He was totally unprepared for it. The fist came flying out of the darkness as he turned the bend in the banister. It struck

92

him on the bridge of his nose. He whirled to face his attacker, reaching for his holstered revolver at the same moment, and suddenly he was struck from behind with something harder than a fist, something that collided with the base of his skull and sent a fleeting wave of blackness across his eyes. He pulled the gun quickly and easily, something else hit him, there were more than two people, again he was struck, he heard his own revolver going off, but he had no knowledge of pulling the trigger. Something dropped to the floor with a clanging metallic sound, they were using pipes, he felt blood trickling into his eye, a pipe lashed out of the near-darkness, striking his mouth, he felt the gun dropping from his hand, felt himself falling to his knees under the steady silent onslaught of the unrelenting lead pipes.

He heard footsteps, a thousand footsteps, running over him and past him and down the steps, thundering, thundering. He did not lose consciousness. With his face pressed to the rough wooden floor, with the taste of his own blood in his mouth, he idly wondered why private eyes always swam down, down, down, into a pool of blackness, wondered idly why Mrs Glennon had lied to him, wondered why he'd been beaten, wondered where his gun was, and groped for it blindly, his fingers sticky with blood. He crawled towards the steps.

He found the top step and then hurtled headlong down the flight, tumbling, crashing into the banister, cutting his bald scalp on the sharp edge of one of the risers, his legs and arms twisted ludicrously as he rolled and bounced to the ground-floor landing. He could see a bright rectangle of light where the vestibule door was opened to the street outside. He spat blood and crawled through the dim vestibule and on to the front stoop, dripping a trail of blood behind him, blinking blood out of his eyes, his nose running blood, his lips running blood.

He half crawled, half dragged himself down the low flight of steps and on to the sidewalk. He tried to raise himself on one elbow, tried to call out to anyone in the street.

No one stopped to assist him.

This was a neighbourhood where you survived by minding your own business.

Ten minutes later a patrolman found him on the sidewalk, where he had swum down, down, down, into that pool of blackness.

The sign outside the garage read BODY AND FENDER WORK, EXPERT PAINTING AND RETOUCHING. The owner of the garage was a man named Fred Batista, and he came out to gas up Brown's unmarked sedan only to learn that Brown was a detective who had come to ask questions. He seemed to enjoy the idea. He asked Brown to park the car over near the air pump and then invited him into the small garage office. Batista needed a shave, and he was wearing grease-covered overalls, but there was a twinkle in his eyes as he and Brown went through the questioning routine. Maybe he'd never seen a cop up close before. Or maybe business was bad and he was glad for a break in the monotony. Whatever the reason, he answered Brown's questions with verve and enthusiasm.

'Joe Wechsler?' he said. 'Why, sure, I knew him. He's got a little hardware store right down the street. Many's the time we run over there when we needed a tool or something. A fine man, Joe was. And a terrible thing what happened to him in the bookstore.' Batista nodded. 'I know Marty Fennerman, too – guy who runs the store. He had a holdup there once, you know that? Did he tell you that?'

'Yes, sir, he told us,' Brown said.

'Sure, I remember, musta been seven, eight years ago. Sure. You want a cigar?'

'No, thank you, Mr Batista.'

'You don't like cigars?' Batista said, offended.

'Yes, I do,' Brown said. 'But I don't like to smoke them in the morning.'

'Why not? Morning, afternoon, what's the difference?'

'Well, I usually have one after lunch and another after dinner.'

'You mind if I smoke one?' Batista asked.

'Go right ahead.'

Batista nodded and spat the end of the cigar into a barrel of soiled rags near his scarred desk. He lighted the cigar, blew out a great stream of smoke, said 'Ahhhhhh', and then leaned back in his ancient swivel chair.

'I understand Mr Wechsler had some work done by you a little while before the shooting, is that right, Mr Batista?'

'That's right,' Batista said. 'A hundred per cent.'

'What kind of work?'

'A paint job.'

'Did you do the job personally?'

'No, no. My body and fender man did it. It wasn't such a big job. Some nut hit Joe while he was parked on the street in front of his store. So he brung the car in here and I—'

'The car was hit?'

'Yeah. But nothing big. You know, just a scratched fender, like that. Buddy took care of it.'

'Buddy?'

'Yeah, my body and fender man.'

'Who paid for the job? Mr Wechsler or the man who hit him?'

'Well, truth is, *nobody* paid for it yet. I just billed Joe last week. 'Course, I didn't know he was gonna get killed. Listen, I can wait for my money. His wife's got enough grief right now.'

'But it was Mr Wechsler you billed?'

'Yeah. Joe didn't know who hit him. Like, you know, he come back from lunch one day, and there was this big scratch in the fender. So he brung the car in here, and we took care of it. Buddy's a good man. Only been with me a month or so, but much better than the last guy I had.'

'I wonder if I could talk to him.'

'Sure, go right ahead. He's out back. He's working on a '56 Ford. You can't miss him.'

'What's his last name?'

'Manners. Buddy Manners.'

'Thanks,' Brown said. He excused himself and walked to the back of the garage.

A tall, muscular man in paint-stained coveralls was spraying the side of a blue Ford convertible. He looked up as Brown approached, decided Brown was no one he knew, and went back to work.

'Mr Manners?' Brown asked.

Manners cut off the spray gun and looked up inquisitively. 'Yeah?'

'I'm from the police,' Brown said. 'I wonder if I could ask you a few questions.'

'Police?' Manners said. He shrugged. 'Sure, go right ahead.'

'You did some work for Joseph Wechsler, I understand.'

'For who?'

'Joseph Wechsler.'

'Wechsler, Wechsler ... oh, yeah, '59 Chevy, that's right. Spray job on the left front fender. Right. I can only remember them by the cars.' He grinned.

'I guess you don't know what happened to Mr Wechsler then.'

'I only know what happened to his car,' Manners said.

'Well, he was killed Friday night.'

'Gee, that's a shame,' Manners said, his face going suddenly serious. 'I'm sorry to hear that.' He paused. 'An accident?'

'No, he was murdered. Don't you read the papers, Mr Manners?'

'Well, I was kind of busy this weekend, I went up to Boston – that's where I'm from originally – to see this girl I know. So I didn't see no papers from here.'

'Did you know Wechsler pretty well?'

Manners shrugged. 'I think I met him twice. First time was when he brung the car in, and then he come in once while I was painting it. Said the colour was a little off. So I mixed a new batch and sprayed the fender again. That was it.'

'Never saw him again?'

'Never. He's dead, huh? That's a shame. He seemed like a nice little guy. For a kike.'

Brown stared at Manners levelly and then said, 'Why do you say that?'

'Well, he seemed nice,' Manners shrugged.

'I mean, why did you call him a kike?'

'Oh. Why, 'cause that's what he was. I mean, did you ever hear him talk? It was a riot. He sounded like he just got off the boat.'

'This spray job you did for him . . . did you argue about the colour of the paint?'

'Argue? No, he just said he thought the colour was a little off, and I said OK, I'll mix a new batch, and that was it. It's hard to match exactly. You know. So I done my best.' Manners shrugged. 'I guess he was satisfied. He didn't say nothing when he picked up the car.'

'Oh, then you did talk to him again?'

'No, I only saw him those two times. But if he'd have kicked about the work, I'da heard it from the boss. So I guess he was satisfied.'

'When did you go to Boston, Mr Manners?'

'Friday afternoon.'

'What time?'

'Well, I knocked off work about three o'clock. I caught the four-ten from Union Station.'

'You go alone, or what?'

'Alone, yeah,' Manners said.

'What's the girl's name? The one in Boston?'

'Why?'

'I'm curious.'

'Mary Nelson. She lives in West Newton. If you think I'm lying about being in Boston—'

'I don't think you're lying.'

'Well, you can check anyway.'

'Maybe I will.'

'OK.' Manners shrugged. 'How'd he get killed? The kike?'

'Someone shot him.'

'That's too bad,' Manners said. He shook his head. 'He seemed like a nice little guy.'

'Yeah. Well, thanks, Mr Manners. Sorry to have interrupted your work.'

'That's OK,' Manners said. 'Any time.'

Brown went to the front of the garage again. He found Batista filling a customer's gas tank. He waited until he was through and then asked, 'What time did Manners leave here Friday afternoon?'

'Two-thirty, three, something like that,' Batista said.

Brown nodded. 'This spray job he did for Wechsler. Did Wechsler complain about it?'

'Oh, only about the first colour Buddy put on. It didn't match right. But we fixed it for him.'

'Any static?'

'Not that I know of. I wasn't here the day Joe came in and told Buddy about it. But Buddy's an easy-going guy. He just mixed up a new batch of paint, and that was it.'

Brown nodded again. 'Well, thanks a lot, Mr Batista,' he said.

'Not at all,' Batista said. 'You sure you don't want a cigar? Go ahead, take one.' Batista smiled. 'For after lunch.'

Carella was downtown at Headquarters watching a parade of felony offenders go through the ritual of the Lineup.

Willis was out talking to known junkies in the neighbourhood, trying to get a lead on the addict named Anthony La Scala.

Di Maeo was rounding up two more known criminals who had been arrested by Bert Kling, convicted, and released from prison during the past year.

Kling was at the funeral parlour with Ralph Townsend, making final arrangements for Claire's burial the next day.

Bob O'Brien was alone in the squad room when the telephone rang. He absent-mindedly lifted the receiver, put it to his ear, and said into the mouthpiece, '87th Squad, O'Brien.' He was in the middle of typing up a report on the results of his barber's shop plant. His mind was still on the report when Sergeant Dave Murchison's voice yanked him rudely away from it.

'Bob, this is Dave downstairs. On the desk. I just got a call from Patrolman Oliver on the South Side.'

'Yeah?'

'He found Meyer beat up on a sidewalk there.'

'Who?'

'Meyer.'

'*Our* Meyer.'

'Yeah, our Meyer.'

'Jesus, what is this? Open season on cops? Where did you say he was?'

'I already sent a meat wagon. He's probably on his way to the hospital.'

'Who did it, Dave?'

'I dunno. Patrolman says he was just laying there in his own blood.'

'I better get over to the hospital. Will you call the loot, Dave? And send somebody up here to cover, will you? I'm all alone.'

'You want me to call somebody in?'

'I don't know what to tell you. There should be a detective up here. You'd better ask the skipper about it. I hate to bust in on a guy's day off.'

'Well, I'll ask the loot. Maybe Miscolo can cover till somebody gets back.'

'Yeah, ask him. What hospital did you say?'

'General.'

'I'll get over there. Thanks, Dave.'

'Right,' Murchison said, and he hung up.

O'Brien put the phone back on to the cradle, opened the top drawer of his desk, took his .38 Police Special from the drawer, clipped it to the left side of his belt, put on his jacket and his hat, made a helpless wide-armed gesture to the empty squad room, and then went through the slatted rail divider and down the iron-rusted steps and past the muster desk where he waved at Murchison, and then out into the October sunshine.

The week was starting fine, all right.

The week was starting just fine.

10

They picked up Terry Glennon at four o'clock. By that time a hardy contingent of bulls had returned to the squad room, and they surrounded Glennon in casual deceptiveness as he sat in a straight-backed chair asking why he had been dragged into a police station.

Bob O'Brien, who was a most obliging cop, said, 'We dragged you into a police station because we think you and some of your buddies beat the crap out of a cop this morning. Does that answer your question?'

'I don't know what you're talking about,' Glennon said.

'The cop's name is Detective Meyer Meyer,' O'Brien went on obligingly. 'He is now at General Hospital being treated for cuts and bruises and shock and maybe concussion. Does that make it any clearer?'

'I still don't know what you're talking about.'

'That's OK; play it cool,' O'Brien said. 'We got all the time in the world. I went to the hospital around lunch time and Meyer told me he had paid a little visit to the Glennon household, where a young guy named Terry Glennon got very upset because Meyer was talking to his mother. The mother, according to Meyer, made some sarcastic reference about the young fellow's friends. Does that ring a bell, Glennon?'

'Yeah, I remember that.'

'How about remembering where you vanished to after you and your buddies ganged up on Meyer?'

'I didn't vanish no place. I was around the block. And I didn't gang up on nobody, neither.'

'You weren't around the block, Glennon. We've been looking for you since noon.'

'So I took a walk,' Glennon said. 'So what?'

'So nothing,' Carella said. 'Fellow can take a walk. No law against that.' He paused, smiled, and said, 'Where'd you go when you left your house, Glennon?'

'Downstairs.'

'Where downstairs?' Willis asked.

'The candy store.'

'What candy store?' Brown asked.

'On the corner.'

'How long did you stay there?' Di Maeo asked.

'I don't know. An hour, two hours, who remembers?'

'Somebody better remember,' O'Brien said. 'Why'd you beat up Meyer?'

'I didn't.'

'Who did?' Carella said.

'I don't know.'

'Ever hear of Claire Townsend?'

'Yes.'

'How?'

'My mother spoke of her. And the cop was asking about her.'

'Ever meet her?'

'No.'

'Know anybody named Joe Wechsler?'

'No.'

'Anthony La Scala?'

'No.'

'Herbert Land?'

'No.'

'Why'd you beat up Meyer?'

'I didn't.'

'Why doesn't your mother like your friends?'

'How do I know? Ask her.'

'We will. Right now we're asking you.'

'I don't know why she don't like them.'

'You belong to a gang, Glennon?'

'No.'

'A club then? What do you call it, Glennon? An athletic and social club?'

'I don't belong to nothing. I don't call it nothing 'cause I don't belong to nothing.'

'Did your gang help you beat up Meyer?'

'I don't have a gang.'

'How many of you were there?'

'I don't know what you're talking about. I went downstairs and—'

'What'd you do? Wait for Meyer in the hallway?'

'—and I stood in the candy store for—'

'Beat him up when he left your mother?'

'—for a few hours, and then I took a walk.'

'Where'd you have lunch?'

'What?'

'Where'd you have lunch?'

'I had a hot dog on Barker.'

'Let's see your hands.'

'What for?'

'Show him your hands!' Carella snapped.

O'Brien turned Glennon's hands over in his own. 'That's all we need,' O'Brien said. 'Those cuts on his knuckles'll cinch it.'

Glennon did not take the bait. He remained silent. If he had been one of the people who'd beaten Meyer with lead pipes, he did not offer the information.

'We're gonna lock you up for a little while,' Willis said. 'I think you'll like our detention cells.'

'You can't lock me up,' Glennon said.

'No? Try us,' Willis answered. 'Steve, I think we better hit the old lady again, find out the names of Junior's friends.'

'You leave my mother alone!' Glennon shouted.

'Why? You gonna beat *us* up, too?'

'You just leave her alone, you hear me? I'm the man of that house! When my father died, *I* became the man of the house! You just stay away from her.'

'Yeah, you're some man,' Brown said. 'You wait in the dark with twelve other guys and you cold-cock a—'

'I didn't wait no place! You just stay away from my mother!'

'Lock him up,' O'Brien said.

'And you can't lock me up, either. You got to have grounds.'

'We got grounds.'

'Yeah? What?'

'Suspicion,' Willis said, calling on the old standby.

'Suspicion of what?'

'Suspicion of being a big shit – how's that? Get rid of him, somebody.'

The somebody who got rid of him was Di Maeo. He pulled him out of the chair, yanking on the handcuffs, and then shoved him through the slatted rail divider and took him downstairs to the detention cells.

'You'd better ask the old lady about this, too,' O'Brien said to Carella. 'Meyer gave it to me at the hospital.'

'What is it?'

O'Brien handed him the page torn from Meyer's pad. It read:

CLAIRE
SATURDAY
271 SOUTH FIRST STREET

Carella read the note: 'Where'd Meyer get this?'

'Hanging on a bulletin board in the Glennon apartment.'

'OK, we'll ask her about it. Anybody checking out this address?'

'I'm going there myself right now,' O'Brien said.

'Good. We'll be with Mrs Glennon. If you get anything, call us there.'

'Right.'

'Does Meyer know who wrote the note?'

'He figures it was the young girl. Eileen Glennon.'

'Why don't we get her in here and ask her about it?'

'Well, that's another thing, Steve. Mrs Glennon says she has a sister in Bethtown, woman named Iris Mulhare.'

'What about her?'

'She claims Eileen went there Saturday morning. She also told Meyer the girl had stayed with Mrs Mulhare all the while the old lady was in the hospital.'

'So?'

'So when I got back to the office, I called Mrs Mulhare. She said yes, the kid was with her. So I said let me talk to her. Well, she hemmed and hawed a little and then told me she was sorry, Eileen must've stepped out for a minute. So I asked her where Eileen had stepped out to. Mrs Mulhare said she didn't know. So I said was she sure Eileen was there at all. She said certainly she was sure. So I said then let me talk to her. And she said, I just told you, she stepped out for a minute. So I told her I thought I'd call the local precinct and send a patrolman over to help find Eileen, and then Mrs Mulhare cracked, and all the dirt came out.'

'Let me hear it.'

'Eileen Glennon isn't with her aunt. The Mulhare woman hasn't seen her for maybe six months.'

'Six months, huh?'

'Right. Eileen isn't there now, and she wasn't there when her mother was in the hospital either. I asked Mrs Mulhare why she'd lied to me, and she said her sister had called that morning – must've been right after Meyer left her – to say, in case anyone asked, Eileen was there in Bethtown.'

'Now why would Mrs Glennon want her to say that?'

'I don't know. But it sure looks as if Claire Townsend was mixed up with a real bunch of prize packages.'

The prize package named Mrs Glennon was out of bed when Carella and Willis arrived. She was sitting in the kitchen drinking a second cup of hot buttered milk, which she'd undoubtedly prepared herself. The neighbourhood grapevine had already informed her of her son's arrest, and she greeted the detectives with undisguised hostility. As if to make her anger more apparent, she slurped noisily at the milk as she answered their questions.

'We want to know the names of your son's friends, Mrs Glennon,' Carella said.

'I don't know any of their names. Terry's a good boy. You had no right to arrest him.'

'We think he and his friends attacked a police officer,' Willis said.

'I don't care what you think. He's a good boy.' She slurped at the milk.

'Does your son belong to a street gang, Mrs Glennon?'

'No.'

'Are you sure?'

'I'm sure.'

'What are his friends' names?'

'I don't know.'

'They never come up here to the house, Mrs Glennon?'

'Never. I'm not going to turn over my parlour to a bunch of young—' She cut herself short.

'A bunch of young what, Mrs Glennon?'

'Nothing.'

'Young *hoodlums*, Mrs Glennon?'

'No. My son is a good boy.'

'But he beat up a cop.'

'He didn't. You're only guessing.'

'Where's your daughter, Mrs Glennon?'

'Do you think *she* beat up a cop, too?'

'No, Mrs Glennon, but we think she had an appointment to meet Claire Townsend on Saturday at this address.' Carella put the slip of paper on the kitchen table, alongside the cup of milk. Mrs Glennon looked at it and said nothing.

'Know anything about that address, Mrs Glennon?'

'No.'

'*Was* she supposed to meet Claire Saturday?'

'No. I don't know.'

'Where is she now?'

'At my sister's. In Bethtown.'

'She's not there, Mrs Glennon.'

'That's where she is.'

'No. We spoke to your sister. She's not there, and she was never there.'

'She's there.'

'No. Now where is she, Mrs Glennon?'

'If she's not there, I don't know where she is. She said she was going to see her aunt. She's never lied to me, so I have no reason to believe—'

'Mrs Glennon, you know damn well she didn't go to your sister's. You called your sister this morning, right after Detective Meyer left here. You asked her to lie for you. Where's your daughter, Mrs Glennon?'

'I don't know. Leave me alone! I've got enough trouble! Do you think it's easy? Do you think raising two kids without a man is easy? Do you think I like that crowd my son runs with? And now Eileen? Do you think I . . .? Leave me alone! I'm sick. I'm a sick woman.' Her voice trailed off. 'Please. Leave me alone. Please.' She was talking in a whisper now. 'I'm sick. Please. I just got out of the hospital. Please. Please leave me alone.'

'What *about* Eileen, Mrs Glennon?'

'Nothing, nothing, nothing, nothing,' she said, her eyes squeezed shut, wailing the words, her hands clenched in her lap.

'Mrs Glennon,' Carella said very softly, 'we'd like to know where your daughter is.'

'I don't know,' Mrs Glennon said. 'I swear to God. I don't know. That's the God's honest truth. I don't know where Eileen is.'

Detective Bob O'Brien stood on the sidewalk and looked up at 271 South First Street.

The building was a five-storey brownstone, and a sign in the first-floor window advertised FURNISHED ROOMS FOR RENT BY DAY OR WEEK. O'Brien climbed the front steps and rang the superintendent's bell. He waited for several moments, received no answer, and rang the bell again.

'Hello?' a voice from somewhere inside called.

'Hello!' O'Brien answered.

'Hello?'

'Hello!' He was beginning to feel like an echo when the front door opened. A thin old man wearing khaki trousers and an undershirt looked out at him. He had shaggy greying brows which partially covered his blue eyes and gave him a peering expression.

'Hello,' he said. 'You ring the bell?'

'I did,' O'Brien answered. 'I'm Detective O—'

'Oh-oh,' the old man said.

O'Brien smiled. 'No trouble, sir,' he said. 'I just wanted to ask a few questions. My name's O'Brien, 87th Squad.'

'How do you do? My name's O'Loughlin, South First Street,' the old man said, and he chuckled.

'Up the rebels!' O'Brien said.

'Up the rebels!' O'Loughlin answered, and both men burst out laughing. 'Come on in, lad. I was just about to have a nip to welcome the end of the day. You can join me.'

'Well, we're not allowed to drink on duty, Mr O'Loughlin.'

'Sure, and who's going to tell anyone about it?' the old man said. 'Come on in.'

They walked through the vestibule and into O'Loughlin's apartment at the end of the hall. They sat in a parlour hung with a coloured-glass chandelier and velvet drapes. The furniture was old and deep and comfortable. O'Loughlin went to a cherrywood cabinet and took out an ornate bottle.

'Irish whisky,' he said.

'What else?' O'Brien asked.

The old man chuckled and poured two stiff hookers. He brought one to O'Brien where he sat on the sofa, and then he sat opposite him in a tall upholstered rocker.

'Up the rebels,' he said softly.

'Up the rebels,' O'Brien answered, and both men drank solemnly.

'What was it you wanted to know, O'Brien?' the old man asked.

'That's got a little bit of a kick,' O'Brien said, staring at the whisky glass, his eyes smarting.

'Mild as your dear mother's milk,' O'Loughlin said. 'Drink up, lad.'

'O'Brien raised the glass cautiously to his lips. Gingerly he sipped at it. 'Mr O'Loughlin,' he said, 'we're trying to locate a girl named Eileen Glennon. We found an address—'

'You came to the right place, lad,' O'Loughlin said.

'You know her?'

'Well, I don't *know* her. That is to say, not personally. But she rented a room from me, that she did.'

O'Brien sighed. 'Good,' he said. 'What room is that?'

'Upstairs. Nicest room in the house. Looks out over the park. She said she wanted a nice room with sunshine. So I give her that one.'

'Is she here now?'

'No.' O'Loughlin shook his head.

'Do you have any idea when she'll be back?'

'Well, she hasn't *been* here yet.'

'What do you mean? You said—'

'I said she rented a room from me, is what I said. That was last week. Thursday, as I remember. But she said she'd be wanting the room for Saturday. Saturday came around, and she never showed up.'

'Then she hasn't been here since she rented the room?'

'Nossir, I'm afraid she hasn't. What is it? Is the poor girl in some trouble?'

'No, not exactly. We just ...' O'Brien sighed and sipped at the whisky again. 'Was she renting the room on a daily basis? Did she just want it for Saturday?'

'Nossir. Wanted it for a full week. Paid me in advance. Cash.'

'Didn't you think it a little odd ... I mean ... well, do you usually rent rooms to such young girls?'

O'Loughlin raised his shaggy brows and peered at O'Brien. 'Well, she wasn't all *that* young, you understand.'

'Sixteen is pretty young, Mr O'Loughlin.'

'Sixteen?' O'Loughlin burst out laughing. 'Oh, now, the young lady was handing somebody a little blarney, lad. She was twenty-five if she was a day.'

O'Brien looked into his whisky glass. Then he looked up at the old man.

'*How* old, sir?'

'Twenty-five, twenty-six, maybe even a little older. But not sixteen. Nossir, not by a long shot.'

'Eileen Glennon? We're talking about the same girl?'

'Eileen Glennon, that's her name. Came here on Thursday, gave me a week's rent in advance, said she'd come by for the key Saturday. Eileen Glennon.'

'Could you ... could you tell me what she looked like, Mr O'Loughlin?'

'I sure can. She was a tall girl. Very big. Maybe five-seven, five-eight. I remember having to look up at her while I was talking. And she had pitch-black hair, and big brown eyes, and—'

'Claire,' O'Brien said aloud.

'Huh?'

'Sir, did she mention anything about another girl?'

'Nope.'

'Did she say she was going to bring another girl here?'

'Nope. Wouldn't matter to me, anyway. You rent a room, the room's yours.'

'Did you tell this to her?'

'Well, I made it plain to her, I guess. She said she wanted a quiet room with a lot of sunshine. The way I figured it, the sunshine was optional. But when somebody comes in here asking for a quiet room, I understand they don't want to be disturbed, and I let her know she wouldn't *be* disturbed. Not by me, anyway.' The old man paused. 'I'm talking to you man to man, O'Brien.'

'I appreciate it.'

'I don't run a cathouse here, but I don't bother my people either. Privacy's a tough thing to find in this city. The way I figure it, every man's entitled to a door he can close against the world.'

'And you got the feeling Eileen Glennon wanted that door to close?'

'Yes, lad, that's the feeling I got.'

'But she didn't mention anyone else?'

'Who else would she mention?'

'Did she sign for the room?'

'Not one of my rules. She paid a week's rent in advance, and I gave her a receipt. That's all she needed. Harry O'Loughlin's an honest man who keeps a bargain.'

'But she never came back?'

'No.'

'Now think hard, Mr O'Loughlin. On Saturday, the day Eileen Glennon was supposed to have taken the room, did . . . did anyone come here asking for her?'

'Nope.'

'Think, please. Did a sixteen-year-old girl come here asking for her?'

'Nope.'

'Did you see a sixteen-year-old girl hanging around outside?'

'Nope.'

'As if she were waiting for someone?'

'Nope.'

O'Brien sighed.

'I don't get it.' O'Loughlin said.

'I think you rented the room to a woman named Claire Townsend,' O'Brien said. 'I don't know why she used Eileen Glennon's name, but I suspect she was renting the room for the young girl. Why, I don't know.'

'Well, if she was renting it for someone else . . . let me get this straight. The girl who rented the room was named Claire Townsend?'

'I think so, yes.'

'And you say she used this Eileen Glennon's name and was actually renting the room *for* her?'

'I think so, yes. It looks that way.'

'Then why didn't Eileen Glennon come here Saturday? I mean, if the room was for her . . .'

'I think she did come here, Mr O'Loughlin. She came here and waited for Claire to pick up the key and let her in. But Claire never showed up.'

'Why not? If she went to all the trouble of renting the room—'

'Because Claire Townsend was killed Friday night.'

'Oh.' O'Loughlin picked up his glass and drained it. He poured himself another shot, moved the bottle towards O'Brien's glass, and said, 'Some more?'

O'Brien covered the glass with his palm. 'No. No, thanks.'

'Something I don't understand,' O'Loughlin said.

'What's that?'

'Why'd Claire Townsend use the other girl's name?'

'I don't know.'

'Was she trying to hide something?'

'I don't know.'

'I mean, was she in trouble with the police?'

'No.'

'Was she doing something unlawful?'

'I don't know.'

'And where'd the other girl disappear to? If she rented the room for her . . .?'

'I don't know,' O'Brien said. He paused and looked at his empty glass. 'Maybe you'd *better* give me another shot,' he said.

The Majesta patrolman had come on duty at four forty-five p.m., and it was now close to six o'clock. It was Indian summer, true, but timetables had no respect for unseasonal temperature and dusk came just as if it were truly autumn. He was walking through a small park, cutting diagonally across it over a path

110

which was part of his beat, when he saw the spot of yellow off under the trees. He peered into the fast-falling darkness. The yellow seemed to be the sleeve and skirt of a topcoat, partially hidden by a large boulder and the trunk of a tree. The patrolman climbed the grassy knoll and walked a little closer. Sure enough, that's what it was. A woman's yellow topcoat.

He walked around the boulder to pick it up.

The coat was thrown carelessly on the ground behind the boulder. A girl was lying on her back not three feet from the coat, staring up at the darkening sky. The girl's eyes and mouth were open. She was wearing a grey skirt, and the skirt was drenched with blood. Dried blood had stained her exposed thighs and her legs. She was no more than sixteen or seventeen years old.

The patrolman, who had seen death before, knew he was looking at a corpse.

He had no way of knowing the corpse was named Eileen Glennon.

11

A corpse has no rights.

If you are a corpse, they can take your picture from a hundred unflattering angles as you stare up unseeingly at the popping flash guns, your skirt pulled back to reveal the dried and caked blood on the inside of your thighs and legs, the last flies of summer swarming about your open mouth. They can press their thumbs into your eyes at last to close your lids, and they can pull your skirt down over your knees and mark the position of your body on the shelf of flat rock where you lay motionless behind the trees. They can roll you on to a stretcher and carry you down to the waiting ambulance, the stretcher bouncing as they move along; they are not concerned for your comfort –

you are beyond feeling. They can put the stretcher down on the floor of the ambulance with a sudden jolt and then cover you with a sheet – your waist, your young breasts, your throat, your face. You have no rights.

If you are a corpse, they can take off your clothing and put it into a plastic bag, and tag it, and send it to the police laboratory. They can place your cold and naked body on a stainless-steel table and dissect you in search of a cause of death. You have no rights. You are a corpse, a stiff, a container of clues perhaps, but no longer a person; you have forfeited your rights – forfeited them to death.

If you are a junkie, you have more rights than a corpse – but not many more.

You can still walk and breathe and sleep and laugh and cry – which is something. These things are life – they are not things to be discounted – and you can still do these things. But if you are a junkie you are involved in your own brand of living death, and you are not very much better off than a bona fide corpse. Your death is continuous and persistent. It starts every morning when you wake up and take that first shot, and it continues throughout the day-long hustle for heroin, punctured by the other death-giving shots, or through the night and into another morning, over and over again, you're a record player spinning the same tired mournful dirge, and the needle is stuck – in your arm. You know you're dead, and everybody else knows it, too.

Especially the cops.

While the corpse named Eileen Glennon was being disrobed and then dissected, a drug addict named Michael Pine was being questioned in the squad room of the 87th Precinct. His questioner was a cop named Hal Willis who could take junkies or leave them alone but whose preference was to leave them alone. A lot has been said about the psychology of the drug addict, but Hal Willis wasn't a psychologist, he was only a cop. He was a disciplined cop who had learned judo because he was only five feet eight inches tall and because he had learned at an early age that big guys like to push around little guys unless little guys learn how to push back. Judo was an exact science and a disciplined one. Drug addiction, so far as Willis was concerned, was the ultimate in lack of discipline. He didn't like junkies, but only because it seemed to him that they didn't *have* to be junkies. He knew with certainty that if he were ever hooked on heroin, he could kick the habit in a week. He would lock himself in a room and puke out his guts, but he would kick it. Discipline. He didn't hate junkies, and he didn't pity them; he simply felt they were lacking in self-control, and this to Willis was unforgivable.

'You knew La Scala, huh?' he said to Pine.

'Yeah,' Pine answered. He delivered the word quickly and curtly. No wise-guy intonation, no enthusiasm, just 'Yeah', like the sharp rap of a knuckle on wood.

'Know him long?'

'Yeah.'

'How long?'

'Two years.'

'He's been a junkie all that time?'

'Yeah.'

'Do you know he's dead?'

'Yeah.'

'Do you know how he died?'

'Yeah.'

'What do you think?'

Pine shrugged. He was twenty-three years old, a blond boy with blue eyes that seemed wide and staring, partially because he'd had a shot before they picked him up and the dilated pupils gave his eyes a weird look and partially because the skin under his eyes was dark, making the blue of the pupils more startling.

'Anybody after him?' Willis asked.

'No.'

'Are you sure?'

'Yeah.'

'Do you know his pusher?'

Pine did not answer.

'I asked you a question. Do you know who La Scala's pusher was?'

'No.'

113

'That's a lie,' Willis said. 'He's probably the same crumb you use.'

Pine still would not answer.

'That's right,' Willis said, 'protect the pusher. That's the smart thing. You scrape together all your nickels and dimes. Go ahead. Make the pusher fat. And then protect him, so he can go right on sucking your blood. You goddamn fool, who's the pusher?'

Pine did not answer.

'OK. Did La Scala owe him any money?'

'No.'

'You sure?'

'You're a cop,' Pine said. 'You know all about how *fat* pushers are, don't you? Then you also know they take cash on the line. No. Tony didn't owe the connection nothing.'

'Got any ideas who killed him?'

'I don't have any ideas,' Pine said.

'You high now?'

'I'm a little drowsy, that's all,' Pine said.

'When did you have your last shot?'

'About an hour ago?'

'Who's your connection, Pine?'

'Aw, come on, cop,' Pine said. 'What's he gonna bother with knocking off a guy like Tony for, huh? That's stupid, ain't it? Would *you* knock off a customer?'

'How bad was Tony hooked?'

'Through the bag and back again.'

'How much did he spend every day?'

'Twenty-five bucks, maybe three bills, maybe more, I don't know. Whatever it was, his connection sure as hell wasn't gonna lose it by knocking him off. Besides, what's the reason?' Pine smiled thinly. 'Pushers *like* hopheads, don't you know that?'

'Yeah, they like 'em,' Willis said dryly. 'All right, tell me everything you know about La Scala. How old was he?'

'About my age. Twenty-three, twenty-four.'

'Married? Single?'

'Single.'

'Parents living?'

114

'I think so. But not here.'

'Where?'

'The Coast, I think. I think his old man is in pictures.'

'What do you mean, pictures? La Scala's father is a movie star?'

'Yeah, just like *my* father is a movie star,' Pine said. 'My father's Cary Grant. You didn't know that?'

'Don't get wise,' Willis said. 'What does La Scala's father do?'

'Something with the crew. A grip, a shmip, who knows? He works with the crew.'

'Does he know his son is dead?'

'I doubt it. Nobody in LA reads newspapers.'

'How the hell would you know?'

'I been West.'

'On your way to Mexico to pick up some junk?'

'What does it matter where I was on the way to? I been West, and in LA nobody reads newspapers. In LA what they do is complain about the smog and keep their eyes open in case Lana Turner should stop for a traffic light. That's what they do out there.'

'You're the first junkie we had in here who's also a social commentator,' Willis said.

'Well, it takes all kinds,' Pine said philosophically.

'So La Scala was living alone, that it?'

'Yeah,' Pine said.

'No girl?'

'No.'

'Did he have relatives besides his parents?'

'A sister, yeah. But she lives on the Coast, too. In Frisco.'

'You think they read the papers there, Pine?'

'Maybe. All I know for sure about Frisco is that all the ladies wear hats.

'You think his sister knows he's dead?'

'I don't know. Give her a call and ask her. You got plenty of taxpayers' money. Give her a call.'

'You seem to be perking up a little, Pine. You're getting a real sharp edge of a sudden.'

115

'Yeah. Well, you can't operate on one level all the time, you know.'

'I wouldn't know. In other words, Pine, La Scala was alone in this city, huh? You know anybody who might have wanted him dead?'

'Nope. Why should they? He wasn't bothering nobody.'

'And all his relatives are in California, is that right, too?'

'That's right.'

'Then nobody here'll miss him,' Willis said.

'I got news for you, cop,' Pine answered. 'Even if they *were* here, they would not miss him.'

Paul Blaney was an assistant medical examiner, a short man with a scraggly black moustache and violet eyes. It was Blaney's contention that he, as junior member on the medical examiner's staff, was always given the most gruesome corpses for necropsy, and he was rather surprised and pleased to receive the body of Eileen Glennon. The girl seemed to be in one piece, and there were no signs of undue violence, no stab wounds, no gunshot wounds, no broken skull. Blaney was sure one of his colleagues had made a mistake in assigning this particular cadaver to him, but he was not a man to look a gift horse in the mouth. Instead, he fell to work with dispatch, half afraid they would change their minds and give him another corpse before he was through.

He called the squad room at one-thirty on Tuesday afternoon, ready to give a full necropsy report to whoever was handling the case. Steve Carella took the call. He had spoken to Blaney many times before, and Blaney was glad that Carella and not another of the 87th's cops had answered the phone. Carella was a man who understood the problems of the medical examiner's office. Carella was a man you could talk to.

The men exchanged the pleasantries and amenities and then Blaney said, 'I'm calling about this little girl they sent over. From what I understand, the body was found in Majesta, but it seems to be connected with a case you're working on, and I was asked to deliver my report to you. I'll send this over typed later, Carella, but I thought you might want the findings right away.'

'I'm glad you called,' Carella said.

116

'Her name's Eileen Glennon,' Blaney said, 'That right?'

'That's right.'

'I wanted to make sure we were talking about the same person before I went through the whole bit.'

'That's OK,' Carella said.

'This was an interesting one,' Blaney said. 'Not a mark on her. Plenty of bloodstains, but no visible wounds. I figure she's been dead a few days, probably since Sunday night sometime. Where was she found, exactly?'

'In a little park.'

'Hidden?'

'No, not exactly. But the park doesn't get much traffic.'

'Well, that might explain it. In any case, I estimate she was lying wherever they found her since Sunday night, if that's any help to you.'

'It might be helpful,' Carella said. 'How'd she die?'

'Well, now, that's what was interesting about this. Does she lived in Majesta?'

'No. She lives with her mother. In Isola.'

'Well, that makes sense, all right. Though I can't understand why she didn't at least *try* to get home. Of course, considering what I found, she probably had a range of symptoms, which could have confused her. Especially after what she'd been through.'

'What kind of symptoms, Blaney?'

'Chills, febrile temperature, vomiting maybe, syncope, weakness, and eventually stupor and delirium.'

'I see,' Carella said.

'The autopsy revealed a slightly distended cervix, tenderness of the lower abdomen, discharge from the external os, and tenacula marks.'

'I see,' Carella said, not seeing at all.

'A septic infection,' Blaney stated simply. 'And, at first, I thought it might have been the cause of death. But it wasn't. Although it certainly ties in with what *did* kill her.'

'And what was that?' Carella asked patiently.

'The bleeding.'

'But you said there were no wounds.'

'I said there were no *visible* wounds. Of course, the tenacula marks were a clue.'

'What are tenacula marks?' Carella asked.

'Tenacula is a plural for tenaculum – Latin,' Blaney said. 'A tenaculum is a surgical tool, a small sharp-pointed hook set in a handle. We use it for seizing and picking up parts. Of the body, naturally. In operations or dissections.'

Carella suddenly remembered that he didn't very often like talking to Blaney. He tried to speed the conversation along, wanting to get at the facts without all the details.

'Well, where *were* these tenacula marks?' he asked pointedly.

'On the cervical lip,' Blaney said. 'The girl had bled profusely from the uterine canal. I also found pieces of pla—'

'What did she die from, Blaney?' Carella asked impatiently.

'I was getting to that. I was just telling you. I found pieces of pla—'

'*How did she die?*'

'She died of uterine haemorrhage. The septicaemia was a complication.'

'I don't understand. What caused the haemorrhage?'

'I was trying to tell you, Carella, that I also found pieces of placental tissue in the cervix of the uterus.'

'Placental . . .?'

'The way I figure it, the job was done either Saturday or Sunday some time. The girl was probably wandering around when—'

'What job? What are you talking about, Blaney?'

'The abortion,' Blaney said flatly. 'That little girl had an abortion some time over the weekend. You want to know what killed her? *That*'s what killed her!'

Somebody had to tell Kling what everybody in the squad room decided that Tuesday. Somebody had to tell him, but Kling was at a funeral. So, instead of speculating, instead of hurling theories at a man who was carrying grief inside him, instead of telling him that one of those closets they'd spoken about had finally been opened and, like all closets opened in the investigation of a homicide, it contained something that should have remained hidden – instead of confronting him with something they knew he would disbelieve anyway – they decided to find out a little more about it. Carella and Meyer went back to see the girl's mother, Mrs Glennon, leaving Bert Kling undisturbed at the funeral.

Indian summer was out of place at that cemetery.

Oh, she had charm, that guileful bitch. The trees lining the road to the burial plot were dressed in gaudy brilliance, reds and oranges and burnt yellows and browns and unimaginable hues mixed on a Renaissance palette. Hotly, they danced overhead, whispering secrets to the balmy October breeze, while the mourners marched beneath the branches of the trees, following the coffin in colourless black, their heads bent, their feet drifting through idle fallen leaves, whispering, whispering.

The hole in the earth was like an open wound.

The grass seemed to end abruptly, and the freshly turned earth began in moist rich darkness, its virgin aroma carried on the air. The grave was long and deep. The coffin was suspended over it, held aloft on canvas straps attached to the mechanism which would lower it gently into the earth.

The sky was so blue.

They stood like uneasy shadows against the wide expanse of sky and the gaudy exhibitionism of the autumn trees. They stood with their heads bent. The coffin was poised for disappearance.

He looked at the black shining box and beyond that to where a man was waiting to release the mechanism. Everything seemed to shimmer in that moment because his eyes had suddenly filled with tears. A hand touched his arm. He turned, and through the glaze of tears he saw Claire's father, Ralph Townsend. The grip tightened on his arm. He nodded and tried to hear the minister's words.

'. . . above all,' the minister was saying, 'she goes to God even as she was delivered from Him: pure of heart, clean of spirit, honest and unafraid of His infinite mercy. Claire Townsend, may you rest in eternal peace.'

'Amen,' they said.

12

Mrs Glennon had had it. She had had it up to here. She didn't want to see another cop as long as she lived. She had identified her daughter at the morgue before they had begun autopsy and then had gone home to put on her widow's weeds, the same black clothing she had worn years ago when her husband had died. And now there were cops again – Steve Carella and Meyer Meyer. Meyer, in true private eye fashion, had swum up out of that pool of blackness, had had his cuts and bruises dressed, and now sat wearing a serious look and a great deal of adhesive plaster. Mrs Glennon faced them in stony silence while they fired questions at her, refusing to answer, her hands clenched in her lap as she sat unflinchingly in a hard-backed kitchen chair.

'Your daughter had an abortion, do you know that, Mrs Glennon?'

Silence.

'Who did it, Mrs Glennon?'

Silence.

'Whoever did it *killed* her, do you know that?'

Silence.

'Why didn't she come back here?'

'Why'd she wander the streets instead?'

'Was the abortionist in Majesta? Is that why she was there?'

'Did you kick her out when you learned she was pregnant?'

Silence.

'OK, Mrs Glennon, let's take it from the top. Did you know she was pregnant?'

Silence.

'How long was she pregnant?'

Silence.

'Goddamn it, your daughter is *dead*, do you know that?'

'I know that,' Mrs Glennon said.

'Did you know where she was going Saturday when she left here?'

Silence.

'Did you know she was going to have an abortion?'

Silence.

'Mrs Glennon,' Carella said, 'we're just going to assume you *did* know. We're going to assume you had foreknowledge that your daughter was about to produce her own miscarriage, and we're going to book you as an accessory before the fact. You better get your coat and hat.'

'She couldn't have the baby,' Mrs Glennon said.

'Why not?'

Silence.

'OK, get your things. We're going to the station house.'

'I'm not a criminal,' Mrs Glennon said.

'Maybe not,' Carella answered. 'But induced abortion is a crime. Do you know how many young girls die from criminal operations in this city every year? Well, this year your *daughter* is one of them.'

'I'm not a criminal.'

'Abortionists get one to four years, Mrs Glennon. The woman who submits to an abortion can get the same prison term. Unless either she or her "quick" child dies. Then the crime is first-degree manslaughter. And even a relative or friend who guided the woman to an abortionist is held guilty of being a party to the crime if it can be shown that the purpose of the visit was known. In other words, an accessory is as guilty as any of the principals. Now how do you feel about that, Mrs Glennon?'

'I didn't take her anywhere. I was here in bed all day Saturday.'

'Then *who* took her, Mrs Glennon?'

Silence.

'Did Claire Townsend?'

'No. Eileen went alone. Claire had nothing to do with any of this.'

'That's not true. Mrs Glennon. Claire rented a room on South First Street, and she used Eileen's name in the transaction. We figure the room was intended for Eileen's convalescence. Isn't that true, Mrs Glennon?'

'I don't know anything about a room.'

'We found the address right here! And the note clearly indicated that Eileen was supposed to meet Claire Saturday. What time were they supposed to meet, Mrs Glennon?'

'I don't know anything about it.'

'Why was it necessary for Eileen to take a furnished room? Why couldn't she come back here? Why couldn't she come home?'

'I don't know anything about it.'

'Did Claire arrange for the abortion?'

Silence.

'She's dead, Mrs Glennon. Nothing you say can hurt her any more.'

'She was a good girl,' Mrs Glennon said.

'Are you talking about Claire or your daughter?'

Silence.

'Mrs Glennon,' Carella said very softly, 'do you think I like talking about abortion?'

Mrs Glennon looked up at him but said nothing.

'Do you think I like talking about pregnancy? Do you think I like invading your daughter's privacy, your daughter's dignity?' He shook his head tiredly. 'A man murdered her, Mrs Glennon. He slaughtered her like a pig. Won't you please help us find him?'

'And do you want more killing?' Mrs Glennon asked suddenly.

'What?'

'Do you want someone else to be killed?'

'What do you mean?'

'You've met my son.' She nodded her head and fell silent again.

'What about him?'

'You see what he did to this fellow here, don't you? And that was only because the man was *questioning* me. What do you think he'd do if he found out Eileen was . . . was—'

'Who are you afraid for, Mrs Glennon?'

'My son. He'd kill him.'

'*Who* would he kill?'

'The . . . the baby's father.'

122

'Who? Who is he?'

'No.' She shook her head.

'Mrs Glennon, we're cops,' Meyer said angrily. 'We're not gonna go telling your son . . .'

'I know this neighbourhood,' Mrs Glennon said wisely. 'It's like a small town. If the police know, everyone will know. And then my son will find the man and kill him. No.' She shook her head again. 'Take me to jail if you want to; hold me as an access . . . whatever you called it. Do that. Say that I murdered my own daughter because I was trying to help her. Go ahead. But I won't have more blood on my hands. No.'

'Did Claire know all this?'

'I don't know what Claire knew.'

'But she did arrange for your daughter to—'

'I don't know what she did.'

'Wouldn't this guy marry your daughter, Mrs Glennon?' Meyer asked.

Silence.

'I'd like to ask one more question,' Carella said. 'I hope you'll give us the answer. I want you to know, Mrs Glennon, that all this embarrasses me. I don't like to talk about it. I don't like to think about it. But I know you have the answer to this question, and I want it.'

Silence.

'Who performed the abortion?'

Silence.

'Who?'

Silence.

And then, out of the silence, suddenly, 'Dr Madison. In Majesta.'

'Thank you, Mrs Glennon,' Carella said softly.

In the car on the long drive to Majesta over the Majesta Bridge, spanning two parts of the city, a bridge as old as time, black and sooty against the sky, squat and sombre in contrast to its elegant rivals, Meyer and Carella speculated on what it all meant.

'The thing I still can't understand,' Carella said, 'is Claire's involvement.'

'Me neither. It doesn't sound like her, Steve.'

'But she sure as hell rented that room.'

'Yes.'

'And she made plans to meet Eileen, so she obviously knew Eileen was going to have an abortion.'

'That's right,' Meyer said. 'But that's what's so contradictory. She's a social worker ... and a *good* one. She knows induced abortion is a felony. She knows if she has anything to do with it, she's involved as an accessory. Even if she didn't know it as a social worker, she certainly knew it as a cop's girlfriend.' Meyer paused. 'I wondered if she ever mentioned this to Bert?'

'I don't know. I think we're gonna have to ask him, sooner or later.'

'I'm not looking forward to it.'

'So ... damn it,' Carella said, 'most social workers *encourage* unwed mothers to have the babies and place them for adoption. Why would Claire ...?'

'The son,' Meyer reminded him. 'A hot-tempered little snot who'd go looking for the father of the child.'

'Claire's boyfriend is a cop,' Carella said flatly. 'She could have prepared us for that eventuality. We could have scared hell out of young Glennon with just a warning to keep his nose clean. I don't understand it.'

'Or, for that matter,' Meyer said, 'why didn't Claire try to contact the father – arrange a marriage? I don't get it. I can't believe she'd get involved in something like this. I just can't believe it.'

'Maybe our doctor friend can shed a little light on the subject,' Carella said. 'What'd the phone book tell us?'

'A. J. Madison, MD,' Meyer said. 'Eleven sixty-three Thirty-seventh, Majesta.'

'That's near that park where they found the girl, isn't it?'

'Yes.'

'You think she'd just come from the doctor's office?'

'I don't know.'

'That doesn't sound likely. She was supposed to meet Claire in Isola. She wouldn't have hung around Majesta. And I doubt if she was sick that soon. Jesus, Meyer, I'm confused as hell.'

'You're just a lousy detective, that's all.'

'I know. But I'm still confused as hell.'

Thirty-seventh Avenue was a quiet residential street with brownstone houses approached by low white stoop fronts and shielded from the sidewalk by low wrought-iron fences. The impression was one of serenity and dignity. This could have been a street in Boston or Philadelphia, a subdued street hidden from the ravages of time and the pace of the twentieth century. It wasn't. It was a street which housed Dr A. J. Madison, Abortionist.

1163 was in the middle of the block, a brownstone, indistinguishable from the brownstones flanking it, the same low iron fence in black, the same white steps leading to the front door, which was painted a subtle green. A rectangular brass plate was set over the brass button. The plate read 'A. J. Madison, MD'. Carella pushed the button. This was a doctor's office, and he didn't have to be told the door would be unlocked. He twisted the huge brass knob and he and Meyer stepped into the large reception room. There was a desk set in one corner before a wall of books. The other two walls were done in an expensive textured wallpaper. A Picasso print hung on one wall, and two Braques were on the other. A low coffee table carried the latest issues of *Life, Look,* and *Ellery Queen's Mystery Magazine.*

'Doesn't seem to be anybody home,' Carella said.

'Nurse is probably out back with him,' Meyer said.

They waited. In a moment they heard cushioned footsteps coming down the long hall leading to the reception room. A smiling blonde entered the room. She wore a white smock and white shoes. Her hair was held tightly at the back of her head in a compact bun. Her face was clean-chiselled, with high cheekbones and a sweeping jawline and penetrating blue eyes. She was perhaps forty years old, but she looked like a young matron, the pleasant smile, the alert blue eyes.

'Gentlemen?' she said.

'How do you do?' Carella said. 'We'd like to see Dr Madison, please.'

125

'Yes?'

'Is he in?' Carella asked.

The woman smiled. 'You don't have an appointment, do you?'

'No,' Meyer said. 'Is the doctor in?'

The woman smiled again. 'Yes, the doctor is in.'

'Well, would you tell him we're here, please?'

'Can you tell me what this is in reference to?'

'Police business,' Meyer said flatly.

'Oh?' The woman's light eyebrows moved ever so slightly. 'I see.' She paused. 'What . . . *sort* of police business?'

'This is a personal matter we'd like to discuss with the doctor himself, if you don't mind.'

'I'm afraid you're talking to "the doctor himself",' the woman said.

'What?'

'*I'm* Dr Madison.'

'What?'

'Yes.' She nodded. 'What is it you want, gentlemen?'

'I think we'd better go into your office, doctor.'

'Why? My nurse is out to lunch, and my next appointment isn't until two o'clock. We can talk right here. I assume this won't take long, will it?'

'Well, that depends . . .'

'What is it? An unreported gunshot wound?'

'It's a little more than that, Dr Madison.'

'Oh?'

'Yes.' Carella took a deep breath. 'Dr Madison, did you perform a criminal abortion on a girl named Eileen Glennon last Saturday?'

Dr Madison seemed mildly surprised. Her eyebrows moved up an eighth of an inch, and the smile came to her mouth again. 'I beg your pardon,' she said.

'I said, Dr Madison, did you perform a criminal abortion on—'

'Yes, certainly,' Dr Madison replied. 'I perform criminal abortions every Saturday. I have special rates for weekend curettage. Good day, gentlemen.'

126

She was turning on her heel when Carella said, 'Hold it right there, Dr Madison.'

'Why should I?' Dr Madison said. 'I don't have to listen to these insults! If this is your idea of a—'

'Yeah, well, you're liable to be a little more insulted,' Meyer said. 'Eileen Glennon is dead.'

'I am very sorry to hear that, but I have no idea *who* the girl is or why you should possibly connect me—'

'Her mother gave us your name, Dr Madison. Now she didn't pick the name out of a hat, did she?'

'I have no idea *where* she picked it – or why. I don't know anyone named Eileen Glennon, and I have certainly never performed a criminal abortion in my life. I have a respectable practice and I wouldn't endanger it for—'

'What's your speciality, Dr Madison?'

'I'm a general practitioner.'

'Must be pretty tough, huh? For a woman doctor to make a living?'

'I do very well, thank you. Your solicitude is wasted. If you're finished with me, I have other things to—'

'Hold it, Dr Madison. Stop running for that back room, huh? This isn't gonna be that easy.'

'What do you want from me?' Dr Madison asked.

'We want you to tell us what happened here Saturday morning.'

'Nothing. I wasn't even *here* Saturday morning. Office hours start at two.'

'What time did Eileen Glennon arrive?'

'I have no idea who Eileen Glennon is.'

'She's the girl you operated on last Saturday,' Meyer said. 'She's the girl who dropped dead of a uterine haemorrhage in the park six blocks from here. That's who she is, Dr Madison.'

'I performed no operation last Saturday.'

'What time did she get here?'

'This is absurd, and a waste of time. If she wasn't here, I'm certainly not going to say she *was*.'

'Did you know she was dead?'

'I didn't even know she was *alive*. I'm sure she was a very nice little girl, but—'

'Why do you call her little, Dr Madison?'

'What?'

'You just called her a nice little girl. Why?'

'I'm sure I don't know. *Wasn't* she a nice little girl?'

'Yeah, but how did you know?'

'How did I know *what*?' Dr Madison said angrily.

'That she was only sixteen years old.'

'I didn't, and I don't. I never heard of Eileen Glennon until just a few moments ago.'

'Didn't you read yesterday's paper?'

'No. I rarely have time for anything but the professional journals.'

'When's the last time you did read a newspaper, Dr Madison?'

'I don't remember. Wednesday, Thursday, I don't remember. I just told you—'

'Then you didn't know she was dead.'

'No. I told you that already. Are we finished now?'

'What time did you operate on her, Dr Madison?'

'I didn't. Nor do I see how you can possibly show that I did. You just told me the girl is dead. *She* can't testify to having had an abortion, and—'

'Oh, she came here alone then, huh?'

'She didn't come here at all. She's dead, and that's that. I never saw her or heard of her in my life.'

'Ever hear of Claire Townsend?' Carella snapped.

'What?'

He decided to take a chance. She had just told him she hadn't seen a newspaper since the middle of last week, before Claire was killed. So, out of the blue, and knowing it was a wild gamble, he said, 'Claire Townsend's still alive. She told us she arranged an abortion for Eileen Glennon. With *you*, Dr Madison. Now how about it?'

The room went silent.

'I think you'd better come downtown and discuss this with Claire personally, huh?' Meyer said.

'I didn't think—'

'You didn't think Claire would tell us, huh? Well, she did. Now how about it?'

'I had nothing to do with the girl's death,' Dr Madison said.

'No. Then who committed the abortion?'

'*I had nothing to do with her death!*'

'Where'd you perform the operation?'

'Here.'

'Saturday morning?'

'Yes.'

'What time?'

'She got here at ten.'

'And you operated when?'

'At about ten-fifteen.'

'Who assisted?'

'I don't have to tell you that. There was a nurse and an anaesthetist. I don't have to tell you who they were.'

'An anaesthetist? That's a little unusual, isn't it?'

'I'm not a butcher!' Dr Madison said angrily. 'I performed the kind of operation she could have got from a gynaecologist in a hospital. I observed every rule of proper aseptic surgical technique.'

'Yeah, that's very interesting,' Carella said, 'since the girl had a septic infection in addition to the goddamn haemorrhage. What'd you use on her? A rusty hatpin?'

'Don't you *dare*!' Dr Madison shouted, and she rushed at Carella with her hand raised, the fist clenched in a hopelessly female attack, her eyes blazing. He caught her arm at the wrist and held her away from him, trembling and enraged.

'Now take it easy,' he said.

'Let go of me!'

'Take it easy.'

She pulled her wrist from his grasp. She rubbed the wrist with her left hand, glaring at Carella. 'The girl had proper care,' she said. 'She was under general anaesthesia for the dilatation and curettage.'

'But she died,' Carella said.

'That wasn't my fault! I told her to go directly to bed when she left here. Instead, she—'

'Instead she *what*?'

'She came back!'

'Here?'

'Yes, *here*.'

'When was this?'

'Saturday night. She told me Miss Townsend hadn't met her where she was supposed to. She said she couldn't go back home, and she begged me to take her in for the night.' Dr Madison shook her head. 'I couldn't do that. I told her to go to a hospital. I gave her the name of a hospital. They would have treated her.' Dr Madison shook her head again.

'She didn't go to any hospital, Dr Madison. She was probably too frightened.' He paused. 'How sick was she when she came here Saturday night?'

'She didn't seem ill. She only seemed confused.'

'Was she haemorrhaging?'

'Of course not! Do you think I'd have let her go if ... I'm a *doctor*!'

'Yeah,' Carella said dryly. 'Who happens to perform abortions on the side.'

'Have you ever carried an unwanted child?' Dr Madison said slowly and evenly. 'I *have*.'

'And that makes everything all right, does it?'

'I was trying to help that little girl. I was offering her escape from a situation she didn't ask for.'

'You gave her escape, all right,' Meyer said.

'How much did you charge for her murder?' Carella said.

'I didn't *murder*!'

'How much?'

'Fi ... five hundred dollars.'

'Where would Eileen Glennon get five hundred dollars?'

'I ... I don't know. Miss Townsend gave me the money.'

'When did you and Claire arrange all this?'

'Two ... two weeks ago.'

'How'd she get on to you?'

130

'A friend told her about me. Why don't you ask *her*? Didn't *she* tell you all this?'

Carella ignored the question. 'How long was Eileen pregnant?' he asked.

'She was in her second month.'

'Then ... since the beginning of September, would you say?'

'Yes, I would guess so.'

'All right, Dr Madison, get your coat. You're coming with us.'

Dr Madison seemed suddenly confused. 'My ... my patients,' she said.

'You can forget all about your patients from now on,' Meyer said.

'Why? What did I do wrong? Try to save a little girl from unwanted misery? Is that so wrong?'

'Abortion is against the law. You knew that, Dr Madison.'

'It shouldn't be!'

'It is. We don't write them, lady.'

'I was helping her!' Dr Madison said. 'I was only ...'

'You killed her,' Meyer said.

But his voice lacked conviction, and he put the handcuffs on her wrists without another word.

FIRST COUNT

The Grand Jury of Majesta, by this indictment, accuse the defendant, Alice Jean Madison, of the crime of abortion, in violation of Sections 2 and 80 of the Penal Law of this state, committed as follows:

The defendant, on or about October 14 at 1163 Thirty-seventh Avenue, Majesta, did unlawfully, feloniously, and wilfully use and employ a certain instrument on Eileen Glennon with intent thereby to procure the miscarriage of said Eileen Glennon, the same not being necessary to preserve the life of the said Eileen Glennon or the life of the child with which she was then pregnant.

SECOND COUNT

The Grand Jury of Majesta, by this indictment, accuse the

*defendant of the crime of manslaughter in the first degree in that
the defendant did unlawfully, feloniously, and wilfully use and
employ a certain instrument on Eileen Glennon with intent
thereby to procure the miscarriage of said Eileen Glennon, the
same not being necessary to preserve the life of the said Eileen
Glennon or the life of the child with which she was then pregnant as a result of all of which she died on October 15.*

*Arthur Parkinson,
District Attorney*

13

Wednesday, October 18.

Indian summer is leaving the city. There is a chill in the squad
room even though the thermostat has been turned up and the
radiators are beginning to clang.

Autumn has arrived suddenly and seemingly without warning. The men sit with their hands wrapped around mugs of hot
coffee.

There is a chill in the squad room.

'Bert, there are some questions we have to ask you.'

'What kind of questions?'

'About Claire.'

The telephone rings.

'87th Squad, Detective Carella. Oh, yes, sir. No, I'm sorry, we
haven't been able to locate them as yet. We're making a routine
check of all pawnshops. Mr Mendel. Yes, sir, as soon as we
have anything. Thank you for calling.'

There was something ludicrous about the scene. Bert Kling
sat in the chair facing the desk. Carella replaced the telephone
in its cradle and then went to stand beside Kling. Meyer sat on
one corner of the desk, leaning over, his elbow cushioned on his

knee. Kling's face was drawn and gaunt. He looked for all the world like a harried suspect being grilled by two hardened detectives.

'What do you want to know?' he asked.

'Did she ever mention Eileen Glennon to you?'

Kling shook his head.

'Bert, please try to think back, will you? This might have been in September sometime, when Mrs Glennon was in the hospital. Did Claire mention having met Mrs Glennon's daughter?'

'No. I would have remembered the minute the Glennons came into the case. No, Steve. She never mentioned the girl.'

'Well, did she ever mention *any* girl? I mean, did she seem troubled about any of her patients?'

'No.' Kling shook his head. 'No, I don't remember, Steve.'

'What did you talk about?' Meyer asked.

'What do you mean?'

'When you were together.'

Kling knew exactly what Meyer was trying to do. He was a cop, and he had used the same technique himself, many times before. Meyer was simply trying to start a train of thought, trying to get words flowing in the hope that they would trigger a significant memory. But, even knowing this, he felt a numbing pain. He did not want to talk about Claire. He did not want to repeat aloud the things they had whispered alone together.

'Can you remember?' Meyer said gently.

'We . . . we talked about a lot of things.'

'Well, like what?'

'Well . . . she had a toothache. This was . . . it must have been the early part of September.'

'Yes, go ahead, Bert,' Carella said.

'And she . . . she was going to a dentist. I remember she . . . she hated it. She . . . she met me one night with her jaw numb. From the novocaine. She asked me to hit her. She . . . she said, "Go ahead, strong man! I'll bet you can't hurt me." She was kidding, you know. Because . . . we had a lot of little jokes like that. You know . . . because I'm a cop.'

'Did she ever talk about school, Bert?'

'Oh, sure,' Kling said. 'She was having a little difficulty with one of her teachers. Oh, nothing like that,' Kling said immediately; 'nothing serious. The instructor had certain ideas about social work, and Claire didn't agree with them.'

'What were the ideas, Bert?'

'I don't remember now. You know how it is in a class. Everybody's got their ideas.'

'But Claire was a *working* student.'

'Yeah. Well, most of the people in the class were. She was doing graduate work, you know. She was going for her master's.'

'Did she ever talk about that?'

'Pretty often. Social work was very important to her, you know.' He paused. 'Well, I guess you don't know. But it was. The only reason we . . . we weren't married yet is because . . . well, you know, she wanted to finish her schooling.'

'Where did you go when you went out, Bert? Any place special?'

'No, just around. Movies, plays sometimes. Dancing. She liked to dance. She was a very good dancer.'

The squad room was suddenly still.

'She was . . .' Kling started and then stopped.

The silence persisted.

'Bert, do you remember any of her ideas about social work? Did she ever discuss them with you?'

'Well, not really. I mean, except where it crossed with police work, do you know what I mean?'

'No.'

'Well, where she was puzzled about a legality. Or where she felt we were doing a bad job. Like with street gangs, you know. She thought we handle them wrong.'

'How, Bert?'

'Well, we're more interested in crime, you know. A kid shoots somebody, we're not too damn interested in the fact that his father's an alcoholic. That's where the social work came in. But she felt social workers and cops should work more closely together. We had a lot of jokes about that, too. I mean, about *us* personally.' He paused. 'I told her all about the P.A.L., and

134

about social workers doing work with street gangs already, but she knew all that. What she wanted was a *closer* working relationship.'

'Had she done much work with young people?'

'Only in connection with her own patients. A lot of people she dealt with had families, you know. So she naturally worked with the kids involved.'

'Did she ever mention a furnished room on South First Street?'

'No.' Kling paused. 'A furnished room? What's this?'

'We think she rented one, Bert. In fact, we *know* she did.'

'Why?'

'To take Eileen Glennon to.'

'Why?'

'Because Eileen Glennon had an abortion.'

'What's Claire got to—'

'Claire arranged for it.'

'No,' Kling said immediately. He shook his head. 'You're mistaken.'

'We've checked it, Bert.'

'That's impossible. Claire would never ... no, that's impossible. She was too aware of the law. No. She was always asking me questions about legal matters. You're wrong. She wouldn't have any part of a thing like that.'

'When she asked about legal matters ... did she ever ask about abortion?'

'No. Why would she ask—?' Bert Kling stopped talking. A surprised look crossed his face. He shook his head once, disbelievingly.

'What is it, Bert?'

He shook his head again.

'*Did* she ask about abortion?'

Kling nodded.

'When was this?'

'Last month sometime. I thought at first ... I thought she was ...'

'Go ahead, Bert.'

'I thought she ... well, I thought it was for herself, you know.

135

But ... what it was ... she wanted to know about *legal* abortions.'

'She asked you that? She asked you when an abortion was considered legal?'

'Yes. I told her only if the life of either the mother or the child was in danger. You know. P.L. 80 – "unless the same is necessary to preserve the life of the woman or of the—"'

'Yeah, go ahead.'

'That's all.'

'Are you sure?'

'No, wait a minute. She asked me a specific question. Just wait a second.'

They waited. Kling's brow knotted. He passed his hand over his face.

'Yeah,' he said.

'What was it?'

'She asked me if the victim of a rape ... a girl who got pregnant because of a rape ... she asked me if the abortion would be legal then.'

'That's it!' Meyer said. '*That*'s what all the goddamn hiding was about! Sure. That's why the furnished room – and that's why Eileen couldn't go home. If the brother ever found out she'd been raped—'

'Hold it, hold it,' Kling said. 'What do you mean?'

'What did you tell Claire?'

'Well, I told her I wasn't sure. I told her it seemed to me that morally it should be permissable to have an abortion in those circumstances. I just didn't know.'

'And what did she say?'

'She asked me to check it for her. She said she wanted to know.'

'Did you check it?'

'I called the D.A.'s office the next day. Preserve the life of the mother or child, they told me. Period. Any other induced abortion would be criminal.'

'Did you tell that to Claire?'

'Yes.'

'And what did she say?'

136

'She blew her stack! She said she thought the law was designed to *protect* the innocent, not to cause them more suffering. I tried to calm her down, you know — what the hell, *I* don't write the laws! She seemed to hold me personally responsible for the damn thing. I asked her why she was getting so excited, and she said something about Puritan morality being the most immoral thing in the world — something like that. She said a girl's life could be completely ruined because she was the victim of a crime and of the law both.'

'Did she ever mention it again?'

'No.'

'Did she ever ask you if you knew any abortionists?'

'No,' Kling paused. 'From what I get . . .' He paused again. 'You think Eileen Glennon was raped, is that it?'

'That's our guess,' Meyer said. 'And probably while her mother was in the hospital.'

'And you think Claire knew about this, and knew she was pregnant, and . . . and arranged an abortion for her?'

'Yes. We're *sure* of that, Bert.' Carella paused. 'She even paid for it.'

Kling nodded. 'I suppose . . . I suppose we could check her bank book.'

'We did that yesterday. She withdrew five hundred dollars on the first of October.'

'I see. Then . . . then I guess . . . well, I guess it's what you say it is.'

Carella nodded. 'I'm sorry, Bert.'

'If she did it, you know,' Kling said, and stopped. '*If* she did it, it was only because the girl had been raped. I mean, she . . . she wouldn't have broken the law otherwise. You know that, don't you?'

Carella nodded again. 'I might have done the same thing,' he said. He did not know if he believed this or not, but he said it anyway.

'She only wanted to protect the girl,' Kling said. 'If you . . . if you look at it one way, she . . . she was actually *preserving* the girl's life, just like the Penal Law says.'

'And in the meanwhile,' Meyer said, 'she was also protecting

137

the guy who raped Eileen. Why does he get out of this clean, Steve? Why does that son of a bitch—'

'Maybe he doesn't,' Carella said. 'Maybe he wanted to do a little protecting of his own. And maybe he started by taking care of one of the people who knew about the rape but who wasn't connected in any personal way.'

'What do you mean?'

'I mean Eileen and her mother wouldn't dare tell about it for fear of what young Glennon would do. But maybe he couldn't be sure of Claire Townsend. So maybe he followed her to that bookshop and—'

'Does the mother know who?' Kling asked.

'Yes, we think so.'

Kling nodded once, tightly. There was nothing in his eyes, nothing in his voice, when at last he spoke.

'She'll tell me,' he said.

It was a promise.

The man lived on the floor above the Glennons.

Kling left the Glennon apartment and began climbing the steps. Mrs Glennon stood in her doorway with her hand pressed to her mouth. It was impossible to know what she was thinking as she watched Kling climb those steps. Maybe she was simply wondering why some people never seemed to have any luck.

Kling knocked on the door to apartment 4A and then waited.

A voice inside called, 'Just a second!'

Kling waited.

The door opened a crack, held by a chain. A man peered out. 'Yes?' he said.

'Police,' Kling said flatly. He held up his wallet, open to his detective's shield.

'What is it?'

'Are you Arnold Halsted?'

'Yes?'

'Open the door, Mr Halsted.'

'What? What is it? Why . . .?'

'Open the door before I bust it in!' Kling answered.

'OK, OK, just a minute.' Halsted fumbled with the chain. As soon as it was loose, Kling shoved the door open and entered the apartment.

'You alone, Mr Halsted?'

'Yes.'

'I understand you have a wife and three children, Mr Halsted. Is that right, Mr Halsted?'

There was something frightening in Kling's voice. Halsted, a short thin man wearing black trousers and a white undershirt, backed away from it instinctively. 'Y ... yes,' he said. 'That's right.'

'Where are they?'

'The children are ... in school.'

'And your wife?'

'She works.'

'How about you, Mr Halsted? Don't you work?'

'I'm ... I'm temporarily unemployed.'

'How long have you been "temporarily unemployed"?' There was a biting edge to Kling's words. He spit them out like razor-sharp stilettos.

'Since ... since last summer.'

'When?'

'August.'

'What did you do in September, Mr Halsted?'

'I—'

'Besides raping Eileen Glennon?'

'Wh ... what?' Halsted's voice caught in his throat. His face went white. He took a step backwards, but Kling took a step closer.

'Put on a shirt. You're coming with me.'

'I ... I ... I didn't do anything. You're mistaken.'

'You didn't do anything, huh?' Kling shouted. 'You son of a bitch, you didn't do anything! You went downstairs and raped a sixteen-year-old girl! You didn't do anything? *You didn't do anything?*'

'Shhh, shhh, my neighbours,' Halsted said.

'*Your neighbours?*' Kling shouted. 'You've got the gall to ...'

139

Halsted backed away into the kitchen, his hands trembling. Kling followed him. 'I ... I ... I ... it was *her* idea,' Halsted said quickly. 'She ... she ... she wanted to. I ... I didn't. It was—'

'You're a filthy lying bastard,' Kling said, and he slapped Halsted openhanded across the face.

Halsted made a frightened little sound, a moan that trembled on to his lips. He covered his face with his hands and mumbled, 'Don't hit me.'

'Did you rape her?' Kling said.

Halsted nodded, his face still buried in his hands.

'Why?'

'I ... I don't know. Her ... her mother was in the hospital, you see. Mrs Glennon. She's ... she's a very good friend of my wife, Mrs Glennon. They go to church together, they belong to the same ... they made novenas together ... they ...'

Kling waited. His hands had bunched into fists. He was waiting to ask the big question. Then he was going to beat Halsted to a pulp on the kitchen floor.

'When ... when she went to the hospital, my wife would ... would prepare food for the children. For Terry and ... and Eileen. And ...'

'Go ahead!'

'I would bring it down to them whenever ... whenever my wife was working.'

Slowly Halsted took his hands from his face. He did not raise his eyes to meet Kling's. He stared at the worn and soiled linoleum on the kitchen floor. He was still trembling, a thin frightened man in a sleeveless undershirt, staring at the floor, staring at what he had done.

'It was Saturday,' he said. 'I had seen Terry leaving the house. From the window. I had seen him. My wife had gone to work – she does crochet beading; she's a very skilled worker. It was Saturday. I remember it was very hot here in the apartment. Do you remember how hot it was in September?'

Kling said nothing in reply, but Halsted had not expected an answer. He seemed unaware of Kling's presence. There was total communication between him and the worn linoleum. He did not raise his eyes from the floor.

'I remember. It was very hot. My wife had left sandwiches for me to take down to the children. But I knew Terry was gone, you see. I would have taken down the sandwiches anyway, you see, but I knew Terry was gone. I can't say I didn't know he was gone.'

He stared at the floor for a long time, silently.

'I knocked when I got downstairs. There was no answer. I . . . I tried the door, and it was open, so I . . . I went in. She . . . Eileen was still in bed, asleep. It was twelve o'clock, but she . . . she was asleep. The cover . . . the sheet had . . . had got . . . had moved down from . . . I could *see* her. She was asleep and I could *see* her. I don't know what I did next. I think I put down the tray with the sandwiches, and I got into bed with her, and when she tried to scream I covered her mouth with my hands and I . . . I did it.'

He covered his face again.

'I did it,' he said. 'I did it, I did it.'

'You're a nice guy, Mr Halsted,' Kling said in a tight whisper.

'It . . . it just happened.'

'The way the baby just happened.'

'What? What baby?'

'Didn't you know Eileen was pregnant?'

'Preg . . . what are you saying? Who? What do you . . .? Eileen. No one said . . . why didn't someone . . .?'

'You didn't know she was pregnant?'

'No. I swear it! I didn't know!'

'How do you think she died, Mr Halsted?'

'Her mother said . . . Mrs Glennon said an accident! She even told my wife that – her best friend! She wouldn't lie to my wife.'

'Wouldn't she?'

'An automobile accident! In Majesta. She . . . she was visiting her aunt. That's what Mrs Glennon told us.'

'That's what she told your wife maybe. That's the story you both invented to save *your* miserable hide.'

'No, I swear!' Tears had welled up into Halsted's eyes. He

reached forward eagerly now, pleadingly, grasping for Kling's arm, straining for support. 'What do you mean?' he said, sobbing. 'What do you mean? Please, oh, please God, no . . .'

'She died getting rid of your baby,' Kling said.

'I didn't know. I didn't know. Oh, God, I swear I didn't—'

'You're a lying bastard!' Kling said.

'Ask Mrs Glennon! I swear to God, I knew nothing about—'

'You knew, and you went after somebody else who knew!'

'What?'

'You followed Claire Townsend to—'

'Who? I don't know any—'

'—to that bookshop and *killed* her, you son of a bitch! Where are the guns? What'd you do with them? Tell me before I—'

'I swear, I swear—'

'Where were you Friday night from five o'clock on?'

'In the building! I swear! We went upstairs to the Lessers'! The fifth floor! We had supper with them, and then we played cards. I swear.'

Kling studied him silently. 'You didn't know Eileen was pregnant?' he said at last.

'No.'

'You didn't know she was going for an abortion?'

'No.'

Kling kept staring at him. Then he said, 'Two stops, Mr Halsted. First Mrs Glennon, and then the Lessers on the fifth floor. Maybe you're a very lucky man.'

Arnold Halsted was a very lucky man.

He had been 'temporarily unemployed' since August, but he had a wife who was an expert crochet beader and willing to assume the burden of family support while he sat around in his undershirt and watched the street from the bedroom window. He had raped a sixteen-year-old girl, but neither Eileen nor her mother had reported the incident to the police because, to begin with, Louise Halsted was a very close friend, and – more important – the Glennons knew that Terry would kill Arnold if he ever learned of the attack.

142

Mr Halsted was a very lucky man.

This was a neighbourhood full of private trouble. Mrs Glennon had been born into this neighbourhood, and she knew she would die in it, and she knew that trouble would always be a part of her life, an indisputable factor. She had seen no reason to bring trouble to Louise Halsted as well – her friend – perhaps her only friend in a world so hostile. Now, with her daughter dead and her son being held for assault, she listened to Bert Kling's questions and, instead of incriminating Halsted in murder, she told the truth.

She said that he had known nothing whatever of the pregnancy or the abortion.

Arnold Halsted was a very lucky man.

Mrs Lesser, on the fifth floor, said that Louise and Arnold had come upstairs at four-forty-five on Friday afternoon. They had stayed for dinner and for cards afterwards. He couldn't possibly have been anywhere near the bookstore where the killings had taken place.

Arnold Halsted was a very lucky man.

All he had facing him was a rape charge – and the possibility of spending twenty years behind bars.

The case was as dead as any of its victims.

The case was as dead as November, which came in with bone-chilling suddenness, freezing the city and its inhabitants, suddenly coating the rivers with ice.

They could shake neither the cold nor the case from the squad room. They carried the case with them all day long, and then they carried it home with them at night. The case was dead, and they knew it.

But so was Claire Townsend.

'It has to be connected with her!' Meyer Meyer said to his wife. 'What else could it be?'

'It could be a hundred other things,' Sarah said angrily. 'You're all blind on this case. It's Bert's girl, and so you've all gone blind.'

Meyer rarely lost his temper with Sarah, but the case was bugging him, and besides, she had overcooked the string beans. 'Who are you?' he shouted. 'Sherlock Holmes?'

'Don't shout at Mommy,' Alan, his oldest son said.

'Shut your mouth and eat your string beans!' Meyer shouted. He turned back to Sarah and said, 'There's too much involved in this! The pregnant girl, the—'

Sarah shot a hasty glance at the children and a warning at Meyer.

'All right, all right,' he said. 'If they don't know where babies come from already, it's time they found out.'

'Where *do* babies come from?' Susie asked.

'Shut up and eat your string beans,' Meyer told her.

'Go ahead, tell her where babies come from,' Sarah said angrily.

'Where, Daddy?'

'It's that women are wonderful, understanding, fruitful, magnificent creatures that God provided for men, you see. And he also made it possible for these lovely, intelligent, sympathetic individuals to be able to make babies, so a man could be surrounded by his children when he comes home from the office.'

'Yes, but where do babies come from?' Susie asked.

'Ask your mother.'

'Can I have a baby?' Susie wanted to know.

'Not yet, dear,' Sarah said. 'Some day.'

'Why can't I have one now?'

'Oh, shut up, Susie,' Jeff, her younger brother by two years, said. 'Don't you know nothing?'

'It's you who don't know nothing,' Susie protested. 'You're not supposed to say "nothing". You're supposed to say "anything".'

'Oh, shut up, you moron,' Jeff said.

'Don't talk to your sister that way,' Meyer warned. 'You

144

can't have a baby because you're too young, Susie. You have to be a woman. Like your mother. Who understands what a man's going through and—'

'I'm simply saying none of you are seeing this thing clearly. You're all involved in a stupid kind of revenge, looking for *any* possible stupid way to tie this in with Claire and blinding yourselves to any other possibility.'

'What possibilities are left, would you mind telling me? We've run this thing into the ground. Not just Claire. Everyone concerned. Everyone. All the victims, *and* their families, *and* their relatives, *and* their friends. There's nothing left, Sarah. So we come right back to Claire and the Glennons, and Dr Madison, and—'

'I've heard this all before,' Sarah said.

'Listen again; it won't kill you.'

'Can I be excused, please?' Alan said.

'Don't you want your dessert?'

'I want to watch "Malibu Run".'

' "Malibu Run" will wait,' Sarah said.

'Mom, it goes on at—'

'It'll wait. You'll have dessert.'

'Let him go if he wants to watch his programme,' Meyer said.

'Look, Detective Meyer,' Sarah said angrily, 'you may be a bigshot investigator who's used to bossing around suspects, but this is *my* table, and I happen to have spent three hours this afternoon preparing dinner, and I don't want my family rushing off to—'

'And burned the string beans while you were doing it,' Meyer said.

'The string beans are *not* burned!'

'They're overcooked!'

'But not burned. Sit right where you are, Alan. You're going to eat dessert if you have to choke on it!'

The family finished its meal in silence. The children left the table, and the sound of underwater mischief came from the living room television set.

'I'm sorry,' Meyer said.

'I am, too. I had no right to interfere with your work.'

'Maybe we *are* blind,' Meyer said. 'Maybe it's sitting there right under our noses.' He sighed heavily. 'But I'm so tired, Sarah. I'm so damned tired.'

CARPENTER

Steve Carella printed the word on a sheet of paper and then studied it. Beneath the word, he printed:

WOODWORKER
CABINETMAKER
SAWYER
WOODSMAN (?)

'I can't think of any other words that mean carpenter,' he said to Teddy. Teddy came to where he was sitting and looked at the sheet of paper. She took it from him and, in her own delicate hand, she added the words: LUMBER? LUMBERMAN? LUMBER-WORKER?

Carella nodded and then sighed. 'I think we're reaching.'

He put the sheet of paper aside, and Teddy climbed on to his lap. 'It probably has nothing to do with the damn case anyway.'

Teddy, watching his lips, shook her head.

'You think it does?' Carella asked.

She nodded.

'It would seem to, wouldn't it? Why else would a guy mention it with his last breath? But ... there are so many other things, Teddy. All this business involving Claire. *That* would seem to be—'

Teddy suddenly put her hands over his eyes.

'What?'

She put her hands over her own eyes.

'Well, maybe we are blind,' he said. He picked up the sheet of paper again. 'You think there's a pun in this damn word? But why would a guy pun when he's dying? He'd tell us just what he was thinking, wouldn't he? Oh, Jesus. I don't know. Let's try breaking it down.' He got another sheet of paper and a pencil for Teddy, and together they began working on possible combinations.

CARPENTER

Carp enter
Car penter
Carpen ter
Carpent, R.

'I'm stuck,' Carella said.

Teddy studied the word list for a moment and then counted the letters in 'carpenter'.

'How many?' Carella asked.

She held up her fingers.

'Nine,' Carella said. 'How does that help us?'

Nine, she wrote on her sheet of paper. *Nein?*

'So?'

She shrugged.

'How about trying it backwards?' Carella said. He wrote down the word: RETNEPRAC. 'That mean anything to you?' he asked.

Teddy studied the word and then shook her head.

'Let's take it from the front again. *Carp.* That's a fish, isn't it?'

She nodded.

'Carp enter. Fish enter. Fish enter. Fishenter. For shenter. Force centre. For centre.' He shrugged. 'You get anything?'

Teddy shook her head.

'Maybe he was trying to tell us that a man named Fish entered the shop and fired those bullets.'

Teddy nodded dubiously.

'Fish,' Carella said. 'Fish enter.' He paused. 'Then why would he say "Carp enter"? Why not simply say "Fish enter"?'

Teddy's hands worked quickly. Carella watched her fingers. *Maybe Willis heard him wrong,* her hands said. *Maybe he was saying something else.*

'Like what?' Carella asked.

She wrote the word on her sheet of paper: CARPETER.

"Like a man who lays carpets?"

Teddy nodded.

'Carpeter.' He thought it over for a moment. 'Maybe.' He shrugged. 'But, then, maybe he was saying "carboner", too.' He could tell by the puzzled look on her face that the words looked alike on his lips: *carpenter, carpeter, carboner*. He moved his paper into place and wrote the word:

CARBONER.

What's a carboner? Teddy's hands asked.

'I don't know,' he said. 'A man who puts carbon on things, I guess.'

Teddy shook her head, a wide grin on her face. *No*, her hands said, *that's the way you Italians say carbon*.

'Atsa right!' Carella said. 'Atsa whatta we say! Carbon-a! Only trouble issa Mr Wechsler, he'sa no was Italian.' He smiled and put down his pencil. 'Come here,' he said. 'I want to discuss this guy who lays carpets.'

Teddy came into his arms and on to his lap.

Neither of them knew how close they'd come.

November.

The trees had lost all their leaves.

He walked the streets alone, hatless, his blond hair whipping in the angry wind. There were ninety thousand people in the precinct and eight million people in the city, and one of them had killed Claire.

Who? he wondered.

He found himself staring at faces. Every passer-by became a potential murderer, and he studied them with scrutiny, unconsciously looking for a man who had murder in his eyes, consciously looking for a man who was white, not short, no scars, marks, or deformities, wearing a dark overcoat, grey fedora, and possibly sunglasses.

In November?

Who?

Lady, lady, *I* did it.

Lady, lady, I fired those guns, *I* left those gaping holes in your side, *I* caused your blood to run all over that bookshop floor, *I* took your life, *I* put you in your grave.

Who?

Who, you son of a bitch?

He could hear his own lonely footsteps echoing on the pavement. The neon clatter was everywhere around him, the sounds of traffic, the sound of voices raised in laughter, but he heard only his own footsteps, their own hollow cadence, and somewhere Claire's remembered voice, clear and vital, even whispering, Claire, Claire, 'Well, I bought a new bra.'

Oh?

'You should see what it does for me, Bert. Do you love me, Bert?'

You know I do.

'Tell me.'

I can't right now.

'Will you tell me later?'

Tears suddenly sprang into his eyes. He felt a loss so total, so complete in that moment, that he thought he would die himself, thought he would suddenly fall to the pavement lifeless. He brushed at his eyes.

He had suddenly remembered that he had not told her he'd loved her, and he would never have the chance to do it again.

It was fortunate that Steve Carella took the call from Mrs Joseph Wechsler. It was fortunate because Bert Kling was very much in sympathy with the woman and had made a few aural adjustments in listening to her. It was fortunate because Meyer Meyer was too accustomed to hearing similar accents and might not have noticed the single important clue she dropped. It was fortunate because Carella had fooled around long enough with the word 'Carpenter' and was ready to pounce on anything that would shed light upon it. The telephone helped. The instrument provided a barrier between the two. He had never met the woman. He heard only the voice that came over the line, and he had to strain to catch every syllable.

'Hallo, dis is Mrs Vaxler,' the voice said.

'Yes, ma'am,' Carella answered.

'From my hosbin is Joseph Vaxler,' she said.

'Oh, yes, Mrs Wechsler. How are you? I'm Detective Carella.'

'Hallo,' she said. 'Mr Carell, I donn like t'bodder you dis way. I know you busy.'

'That's quite all right, Mrs Wechsler. What is it?'

'Vell, ven your d'tectiff vas here, I gave him a bonch bills he said he vanted t'look oveh. I need them beck now.'

'Oh, I'm terribly sorry,' Carella said. 'They should have been returned to you long ago.'

'Dot's ull right,' Mrs Wechsler said. 'I vouldn't be boddering you, but I got today a second bill from d'men vot pented the car, and I remembered I didn't pay yet.'

'I'll see that they're sent to you right away,' Carella said. 'Somebody up here must have goofed.'

'Thank you. I vant to pay them as soon as—'

'The what?' Carella said suddenly.

'Pardon?'

'The what? The man who *what*?'

'I donn know vot you mean, Mr Carell.'

'You said something about a man who—'

'Oh, d'car penter. The men vot pented Joseph's car. Dot's right. Dot's who I got d'second bill from. Vot abodd him?'

'Mrs Wechsler, did ... did your husband talk the way you do?'

'Vot?'

'Your husband. Did he ... did he sound the way you do?'

'Oh, voise, d'poor men. But he vas good, you know. He vas a dear, good—'

'Bert!' Carella yelled.

Kling looked up from his desk.

'Come on,' Carella said. 'Goodbye, Mrs Wechsler, I'll call you back later.' He slammed the phone on the hook.

Kling was already clipping on his holster.

'What is it?' he said.

'I think we've got him.'

15

Three cops went to make the collar, but only one was needed.

Brown, Carella, and Kling talked to Batista, the owner of the garage. They talked in quiet whispers in the front office with the scarred swivel chair. Batista listened with his eyes wide, a cigar hanging from one corner of his mouth. Every now and then he nodded. His eyes got wider when he saw the three detectives draw their revolvers. He told them where Buddy Manners was, and they asked him to stay right there in the front office until this was all over, and he nodded and took the cigar out of his mouth and sat in the swivel chair with a shocked expression on his face because television and the movies had suddenly moved into his life and left him speechless.

Manners was working on a car at the back of the garage. He had a spray gun in his right hand, and he was wearing dark glasses, the paint fanning out from the gun, the side of the car turning black as he worked. The detectives approached with guns in their fists, and Manners looked up at them, seemed undecided for a moment, and then went right on working. He was going to play this one cool. He was going to pretend that three big bastards with drawn guns always marched into the garage while he was spraying cars. Brown was the first to speak; he had met Manners before.

'Hello there, Mr Manners,' he said conversationally.

Manners cut off the spray gun, pushed the dark glasses up on to his forehead, and squinted at the three men. 'Oh, hello,' he said. 'Didn't recognize you.' He still made no mention of the hardware, which was very much in evidence.

'Usually wear sunglasses when you're working?' Brown asked conversationally.

'Sometimes. Not always.'

'How come?'

'Oh, you know. Sometimes this stuff gets all over the place. When I've got a small job, I don't bother. But if it's anything

151

big I usually put on the glasses.' He grinned. 'Be surprised how much wear and tear on the eyeballs it saves.'

'Mmm-huh,' Carella said pleasantly. 'Ever wear sunglasses in the street?'

'Oh, sure,' Manners answered.

'Were you wearing them on Friday, October 13?' Carella asked pleasantly.

'Gee, who knows? When was that?'

'The middle of last month,' Carella said pleasantly.

'Maybe, who knows? We had a lot of sunshine last month, didn't we? I could've been wearing them.' He paused. 'Why?'

'Why do you think we're here, Mr Manners?'

Manners shrugged. 'I don't know. Stolen car? That it?'

'No, guess again, Mr Manners,' Brown said.

'Gee, I don't know.'

'We think you're a murderer, Mr Manners,' Carella said.

'Huh?'

'We think you went into a bookstore on Culver Avenue on the evening of—'

And Kling suddenly reached for him. He stepped between Brown and Carella, cutting off Carella's words, grabbing Manners by the front of his coveralls and then pushing him backwards against the side of the car, slamming him there with all the strength of his arm and shoulder.

'Let's have it,' Kling said.

'Let's have what? Let go of my—'

Kling hit him. This was not a dainty slap across the cheek nor even a vicious backhanded swipe to the jaw. Kling hit him with the butt of his .38. The gun collided with Manners' forehead, just over his right eye. It opened a cut two inches long which began bleeding immediately. Whatever Manners had expected, it wasn't this. He went dead white. He shook his head to clear it and then stared at Kling, who hulked over him, right hand holding the gun, poised to strike again.

'Let's have it,' Kling said.

'I . . . I don't know what—'

Kling hit him again. He swung up his arm, and then he

152

brought it forward and down in a sharp short blow, hitting the exact same spot, like a boxer working on an opened wound, hitting directly and with expert precision, and then pulling back the gun, and tightening his left hand in Manners' clothes, and saying, 'Talk.'

'You son of a . . . you son of a bitch,' Manners said, and Kling hit him again, breaking the bridge of his nose with the gun this time, the bones suddenly splintering through the skin.

'Talk,' he said.

Manners was bellowing in pain. He tried to bring his hands to his shattered nose, but Kling shoved them away. He stood before the man like a robot, the hand tight in the front of the coveralls, his eyes slitted and dead, the gun ready.

'Talk.'

'I . . . I . . .'

'Why'd you do it?' Kling asked.

'He . . . he . . . oh, Jesus, my nose . . . Jesus, Jesus, Jesus . . .' The pain was excruciating. He gasped with the agony of trying to bear it. His hands kept flitting up to his face, and Kling kept knocking them away. Tears filled his eyes mixed with the blood from the open wound on his forehead, running into the blood that gushed from his mashed nose. Kling brought back the gun a fourth time.

'No!' Manners screamed. '*Don't!*' And then the words came streaming from his mouth in an anxious torrent, tumbling from his lips before the gun descended again, one word piling on to the next, a hysterical outburst from a terrified and wounded animal. 'He came in here the lousy Jew bastard and told me the colour was wrong the lousy kike told me the colour was wrong I wanted to kill him right then and there I had to do the whole job over again the lousy son of a bitch bastard he had no right telling me the kike the louse I told him I warned him I told him he wasn't going to get away with this can't even speak English the bastard I followed him I killed him I killed him I killed him *I killed* him!'

The gun descended.

It hit Manners in the mouth and shattered his teeth, and he

collapsed against the car as Kling raised the gun again and fell upon him.

It took both Carella and Brown a full five minutes to pull Kling off the other man. By that time, he was half dead. Carella was already typing up the false report in his head, the report which would explain how Manners had resisted arrest.

Patterns.

Indictment for Murder in the First Degree by Shooting

FIRST COUNT

The Grand Jury of Isola, by this indictment, accuse the defendant of the crime of murder in the first degree, committed as follows:

The defendant in Isola, on or about October 13, wilfully, feloniously and of malice aforethought shot Herbert Land with a pistol and thereby inflicted divers wounds upon said Herbert Land and thereafter and on or about October 13 said Herbert Land died of the wounds.

SECOND COUNT

. . . feloniously and of malice aforethought, shot Anthony La Scala with a pistol and thereby inflicted divers wounds . . .

THIRD COUNT

. . . upon said Joseph Wechsler and thereafter and on or about October 13 . . .

FOURTH COUNT

. . . said Claire Townsend died of the wounds.

Patterns.

The pattern of December sunlight filtering past barred and grilled windows to settle in a dead white smear on a scarred wooden floor. Shadows merge with the sun smear, the shadows of tall men in shirt sleeves; it will be a cold December this year.

A telephone rings.

There is the sound of a city beyond those windows.

'87th Squad, Carella.'

There are patterns to this room. There is a timelessness to these men in this place doing the work they are doing.

They are all deeply involved in the classic ritual of blood.

Ed McBain

Hail to the Chief 80p

Carella looked into the frozen ditch as Kling fanned his flashlight over
the naked bodies. Who was responsible? The Death's Heads, the
Scarlet Avengers or the Yankee Rebels? A couple of detectives with six
corpses on their hands needed all the help they could get, and they
wouldn't get it from the gangs, that was sure . . .

Blood Relatives 70p

Saturday night, and party night on the Precinct – the perfect backdrop
for a knife-carrying sex attacker. Seventeen-year-old Muriel was
stabbed to death and her cousin Patricia got away with a slashed cheek.
When she ran into the station house Kling watched the bloody hand-
prints appear on the glass panel. A messy start to a case that got
messier – every time Patricia changed her story . . .

'Totally gripping . . . he rivets the reader throughout'
JILL NEVILLE, BBC KALEIDOSCOPE

Sadie When She Died 80p

The police photographer made sure Sarah Fletcher looked as good as
any lady *can* look with her belly slashed open and her guts on the
bedroom rug. Gerald Fletcher called his wife a no-good bitch. Why was
he so glad someone had murdered his wife?

Detectives Kling and Carella found the answer in Sarah's little black
book – the amatory exploits of Sadie Collins . . .

'Reveals McBain as a transatlantic Simenon' GUARDIAN

Ed McBain

So Long As You Both Shall Live 80p

Wedding bells on the 87th Precinct on a bleak November Sunday. The photographer had never seen so many cops in his life. Not surprising, considering that the bridegroom was Detective Kling, his bride the lovely Augusta. But those off-duty cops weren't celebrating for long: with the reception over, Kling's bride was snatched from the honeymoon suite...

'The best of today's procedural school of police stories'
NEW YORK TIMES

Jigsaw 80p

There's nothing like a little homicide to give the 87th Precinct a shot in the arm. Or the chest, as the case may be... Detectives Brown and Carella had themselves a puzzle with six missing pieces. Put it together and there's $750,000 for the taking. In this case bodies were easy to find – clues came a little harder...

'McBain's so far ahead of police-procedural writers that its virtually a one-horse race... Hyper-readable, witty, credible' SCOTSMAN

Let's Hear It for the Deaf Man 70p

If you happen to be a cop, there are some people you don't need – like a guy with an arrow in his chest, a burglar who leaves a kitten as his calling-card, a hippie crucified on a tenement wall – and the Deaf Man, who announced he was going to steal half-a-million dollars then needled Steve Carella with a series of cryptic picture clues.

'... the climax is ecstatically satisfying' OBSERVER

Agatha Christie
The Big Four 90p

'Li Chang Yen is the controlling force. I have designated him Number One. Number Two is represented by the sign for a dollar. Number Three is a woman, her nationality French. Number Four . . .' The voice faltered and broke . . . Four ruthless criminals seek world domination. Between them and their goal stands one man – the inimitable Hercule Poirot!

'The acknowledged queen of detective fiction' OBSERVER

Leslie Thomas
That Old Gang of Mine £1.25

Meet ODDS – the Ocean Drive Delinquent Society – a band of geriatric drop-outs chasing excitement and danger in their twilight years in the Florida sun. There's Ari the Greek, K-K-K-K-Katy the dancing queen, Molly Mandy who supplies the gang's arms cache (and one and only bullet), and ex-hood Sidewalk Joe.

Hot on their heels comes the baffled Salvatore, local police captain, and bumbling private eye Zaharran. Never was organized crime so disorganized.

'Hilarious' DAILY MIRROR

Patrick Alexander
Show Me a Hero £1.25

Into the 1980s, a tyranny of the left rules Britain with Saracen troop carriers, while propaganda cloaks the corpses. Backs to the wall, the Resistance plans Operation Volcano, while up at the sharp end of every strike is the man they call the Falcon – a Robin Hood with an Uzi machine-gun and nerves of steel. One of nature's heroes, temporarily useful, ultimately expendable . . .

'Probably very near the truth' YORKSHIRE POST